L. BLANKENSHIP

This book is a work of fiction. All the characters and events portrayed in this book are ficticious, and any resemblance ro real people or actual events is purely coincidental.

DISCIPLE, PART I

©2012 by L. Blankenship

Edited by Debra Doyle
Cover artwork by Faiz Nabheebucus
Maps by The Cabil
Cover design by The Cabil
Published by The Cabil

discipleofthefount.blogspot.com/

ISBN: 978-0-9664765-3-8
Third printing.

This book could not have happened without those who
supported my Kickstarter project:
Laura Bergstresser
Stephanie Charette
Sarah Goslee
Chris Ingram
Thomas & Mona Jensen
Shawn McDonald
Lauren Teffeau
Elizabeth Twist
Zorlond

Also by L. Blankenship

Novels/Novellas

Disciple, Part I
Disciple, Part II
Disciple, Part III

Fire's First Kiss

Anthologies

The Battle of Ebulon

DISCIPLE, PART I
for want of a piglet

CHAPTER 1

"You couldn't sleep either?"

At the whisper, I looked up from struggling to lace my boots with trembling hands. My master stepped into my dormitory room, adding his lamp's light to my candle.

"Why must I dress as a boy?" I whispered back. Perhaps I was not so buxom, but I doubted I'd fool anyone. "This makes little sense."

"Patience." Master Parselev placed his lamp on my writing-table and checked my packed bags. "They're gathering at the chapel already. None of us got much sleep, it seems."

The straw mattress creaked when I stood, boots laced and the woolen hose sagging between my thighs. I ran my fingers around my waist, under my layered cotes, to check the drawstring. "Are these right, Master?" I'd strung the hose and braies together as best I could guess and as memory was my Blessing I had no excuse for failing. Men's underthings weren't much concern to me — if I saw such, or more, it was while the man lay bleeding on the surgery table.

"If they stay up, it's right. Good. This too." He slung a heavy felt cloak across my shoulders and pinned it on. The hood buried my face in shadows; my blonde braid, even wrapped around my head, would give me away.

I asked, "Master, this journey will be long, won't it?" Parselev had given me more clothes than I'd ever owned to pack in those bags. All heavy winter woolens, too. "Shouldn't you go, then?"

He looked down at me, mouth quirking to one side. Master was a greybeard, said to be over a hundred years old, but his kir kept his eyes bright and his face lightly creased. I had only been his apprentice two years. Surely I could not be ready for this.

"It must be you, Kate," was all he said. He carried one of my bags, and I took the other.

Wreathed in breath-clouds, we crossed the Order's campus. Low on the horizon, the slim, waxing crescent of the Shepherd hung golden, all seven of his Flock scattered in the sky behind him. He gave the only hint that dawn was coming. The cloak kept me marvelously warm, even in the chilly breeze. No frost this morning, not yet, but it was only a few weeks off.

Master un-bolted the side gate and led me to the door of the Grand Chapel. Horses waited on the grass, many horses chewing at their bits and shaking their heads, most of them with knights in the saddles. The knights' black tabards, worn over suits of mail, had a white horse embroidered on the right shoulder and two gold stars on the left, marking them knights and Prince's Guard as well. Kite shields and bucket helms hung on their saddles, in easy reach.

Several of the horses stood with empty saddles, collectively held by a couple of pageboys, and that gave me pause. I'd never been on a horse; I was only a peasant girl. But it could not be so awful, I told myself, so I gripped my cloak a little tighter and followed Master Parselev inside.

My new boots rang too loudly in the empty chapel, and when I slowed to lighten my step I fell behind. Only one lamp burned on the high table before the icons, and its light was mostly blocked by those gathered below the two steps. Faces were cast in shadow as they turned toward us — all looming in the dim light, some cloaked like me, others not — and I knew none of them. I kept my head down as I joined my master before them, glad the hood hid my face.

"Not ready, Elect?" one asked, his voice low but strong. "Who's this?"

"My apprentice will safeguard the travelers," my master answered. "She has —"

"What?" The man stepped closer, his shoulders blocking out the light.

"Majesty, she's my finest student." Parselev put up a hand when the stranger reached for my hood.

My knees trembled as the word echoed in my head. Majesty. I stood before the king of Wodenberg. Wobbling a bit, I dropped to one knee in obeisance, fist pressed to my heart. The king yanked off my hood while I stared at the flagstone floor, pulse pounding.

"This girl?" the king demanded. "You trust a mere disciple with this mission?"

"Absolutely. Saint Qadeem and I have discussed it, and we agree. Do we not, Master?"

"We are in agreement, Wilhelm." I felt kir blossom nearby, like a candle flaring to life in a dark room, and my own kir stirred in my chest. He was here, no doubt, my master's master. Our saints appeared and spoke to us on solstices, and I knew that silken, lilting voice. My saint, the one who'd Blessed me with perfect memory and marked me as his disciple. Kings and now saints in the chapel, and me just a peasant-born apprentice. I didn't dare budge.

"You know what rides on this mission," King Wilhelm said.

"And know well," Saint Qadeem replied. "Accord her the proper rank of a physician and let her take her place. Kate?"

I hesitated, even then. "M'lord?"

Gently, "Stand up, Kate Carpenter."

Hands clenched on the felt cloak, I managed to rise and risked a glance at the high table before the icons of the Mother and the Father. All three saints were there, jolting cold terror through my veins. Qadeem sat in the middle, olive-skinned and exotic as his voice. His kir-lit eyes glittered black as midnight. I could see nothing else.

He spoke with a faint, kind smile. "It's not the Saint-day announcement and not the celebration feast that a new physician deserves. But once it's done it's done. I ask believing that you will not fail me, Kate. Do you accept the duties and the burdens of Physician as my disciple?"

Even though my voice quavered, I raised my chin. "I am honored to."

<hr/>

King Wilhelm put a strong hand on my shoulder and charged me with the care of those assigned to this mission. It so stunned me that I stared up at him, forgetting myself, for a moment. Then he patted me, heavy as a brick, and stepped away.

The three saints came down from the high table to lay hands on their disciples and say a few words. Saint Woden went to the two cloaked men who wore swords — they were surely his disciples. Saint Aleksandr the craftsman spoke to the two others briefly, clasping each by the hand. Qadeem went first to one of Aleksandr's disciples.

I stood alone for a moment; the king and an armed woman had drawn Master Parselev aside. Her black tabard, over the mail, bore four gold stars and captain's brasses; someone had told me the captain of the King's Guard was a woman. She studied me and I fidgeted with my cloak.

I was a newly minted physician and an honorary knight as well. My master and saint thought me ready to serve the kingdom. Surely she'd been as eager, once. I would do my duty, whatever my saint asked.

A light hand on my shoulder. Saint Qadeem was not so tall, I realized as I turned, and not so broad-shouldered. I'd never been so near to him. His hair was as inky black as his eyes and his hands deft when he straightened my cloak. They warmed my cheeks when he cupped my face briefly, and kir tingled into me through his touch. It swirled and settled in my chest, soothing and cheering.

With a crisp nod, he pulled my hood back up.

No more needed saying to me, it would seem. Though I wanted to ask him why.

My new companions — those in the cloaks like me, I had to guess — strode out to where the horses waited. I followed, my eyes feeling dry but I still could not blink as I stood looking at the horses. They looked back, breath billowing around their heads. The four hooded men chose their mounts and swung up into the saddles, one of them pausing again to speak quietly with the king and the captain of the guard.

"Kate, I put this together for you." Master Parselev emerged last from the chapel with a bulging messenger bag in his hand. He passed it too me by the strap, and for all its bulk it wasn't heavy. "Well stocked for first aid. Charms, too."

"Where are we going? How far? We'll be home before the frost, won't we?"

"Your leader will tell you soon enough. For now, keep your hood up." My master smiled, but it thinned under his worry. "Onto the horse with you." He turned and saw that one of my new companions waited with two horses' reins in hand.

"I've never been on a horse."

"Pal, then," the man said, turning to the horse on his right. "I'm Ilya, m'lady. Ilya Rabskov."

"I'm Kate Carpenter."

"Dame Kate," my master corrected. I must've looked bewildered, because he reminded me, "You've been knighted by the king. Dame Kate."

Ilya showed me how to wedge my foot in the stirrup and helped boost my rump up into the saddle. While he checked that my other foot was well in, he told me, "Just let Pal follow the others. He won't give you any trouble."

I heard a whistle and twisted in the saddle to see the two knights — armed, mailed, though I didn't catch the insignia on their tabards — tap their horses to a trot. Our third companion rode after. Pal's ears pricked up and he seemed glad to follow. Ilya was quick to mount up and join me.

I glanced back toward the chapel as the twenty-odd knights of the Prince's Guard fell in behind. Master Parselev, the king, and the captain of the King's Guard watched us go, hard to spot in the chilly shadows of dawn.

———————————✠———————————

Our two leaders took us out of the Order by the main gate and we rode down River Road at a quick walk.

"Ther Boristan Tolstyev," the third of our party introduced himself. "Glad to meet you, Dame Kate. Took you by surprise, did they?" He was Russe, like Ilya: thick-handed, barrel-chested, on the rusty side of blond. Honest, sober faces, and the Ther's bearded as well.

"Easy, easy," Ilya said, reaching over to tug on Pal's reins for me. "Don't squeeze. He'll think you want him to run."

From the height of a saddle, I wouldn't want to go any faster down a slope like River Road's. It was all I could do to cling to Pal. "Mother's mercy, no," I breathed. I already rocked far too much, it seemed.

5

Pal slowed a bit, though we'd gotten closer to the pair in the lead. My pulse eased enough to answer Ther Boristan. "Yes, a surprise. Master Parselev brought me a whole wardrobe and Ter Holly helped me pack last night. That was the first I—"

The tallest horse, the grey, slowed alongside me until the rider's stirrup knocked against mine. The knight's hood, pulled deep, shadowed his face completely. Pointing to the two men, our leader said, "Keep your voices down. We're eastbound to reinforce Baron Eismann against the harriers Arcea's sent across the Wall. That's all you need say to anyone. And you." The finger turned to me and his tone sharpened. "Not a word." At a tap, the grey stepped ahead to the lead.

His black tabard, under the cloak, bore the royal sigil, a full Shepherd moon silhouetting Mount Woden. Only the king and the prince wore it. Stung, I set my teeth on my lower lip. Kings, saints and princes. My mother would never believe this, if I lived to tell it.

Ilya leaned over to put my hands on the saddle horn, which improved my stability without squeezing Pal with my knees. I was grateful for that much.

Even so early, on a dew-laden morning, wagons and riders plied River Road. The Shepherd's thin crescent faded into the strengthening dawn and the small Flock moons turned from ivory to gold. Wodenberg's city gate stood open and we rode through with hardly a glance from the armsmen on duty. True to its name, River Road sloped onward through the grassy Spanne that ringed the city wall, and the foulburg below, to the Neva. The water rippled, languorous, as the early ferry crept its way along the guide-rope.

We turned onto the Southbound Road and wove through a cluster of wagons stacked with sheaves of oats. The sliver of the Shepherd signaled the start of the Grain Moon and the harvest in earnest. The rumbling hooves of the Prince's Guard held many eyes as we passed, but knights a-horse were not so uncommon, these days.

Arcea's harriers troubled the southlands; I'd heard the stories as much as anyone. There'd been little good news since the disaster at Ansehen a moon and a half ago. Master Parselev had taken me to assist him in the surgery — my first trial by fire, and the same for many young knights. It had been a terrible battle. Arcea had sent an elect, a kir-mage who ranked just below the saints themselves, and

King Wilhelm spent many lives to break through the enemy line. With Saint Woden's aid, the elect was killed.

The earthquake called up in the final duel destroyed Ansehen. The castle and the gates that barred the Southbound Road cracked and tumbled. I had seen it myself.

Without their elect, and suffering losses thanks to the prince's cavalry charge, Arcea's army withdrew. The word was that their general swore to return in the spring. Arcea was a huge empire, and had armies and elect to spare.

Wodenberg's knights and infantry had paid heavily, too, and ours was a far smaller kingdom.

My thoughts trailed off, though, as we hurried past inns and taverns and wagon yards. Soon the buildings thinned out, spread by small pastures at first and then stone-walled oat fields. I'd been born in Wodenberg city and never been further than the river's shore. But still our leader rode on, silent and cloaked.

Pal's easy walk and the warm sun lulled me, even in the saddle. Ilya had passed me a trail biscuit and a waterskin to wash it down. We'd picked up to a canter for some distance, and I'd nearly fallen for not knowing what to do, but Ilya caught me, Father bless him, and helped me get the rhythm. I caught sight of the earthwork fortress where the Felsherz met the Neva as we turned off the Southbound Road onto an eastbound branch. After the terror of cantering wore off, the sleep I'd missed put me in a doze until a sharp whistle jerked me awake.

A column of black smoke marred the blue sky, freshly sprung from somewhere on the road ahead.

A Guard with captain's brasses on his epaulettes had joined the prince and the second knight of our company at the head of our party. The captain twisted in his saddle and shouted back, "Brauer, escort them!" while pointing at Ther Boristan, Ilya and me. Then they were off at a canter and the mass of Prince's Guard flowed around me for a moment. Pal perked up and wanted to run too, but I pulled on the reins. Maybe too hard; he fretted a bit, tossed his head.

"Easy on him," Ilya told me.

The horses kicked up dirt in pulling away from us. Sergeant Brauer and his squad of five stood with us on the road. The men shielded their eyes against the morning sun.

"Is it Gabel?" one of the squad asked.

"I'd bet it," Brauer answered. "Got some stones on them, to raid this close to the city."

"M'lord'll straighten them on that," another knight said. After a few heartbeats of watching the smoke climb, he said, "Must be worse in the hills if we're reinforcing Baron Eismann."

We rode in at a walk and when we reached Gabel there were only a handful of dead Arceal soldiers and a half dozen Prince's Guard securing the town square after the fight. The smoke came from the fields south of the small town — a handful of houses, an inn, a tavern and an Orderhaus — and it thinned as we watched.

I swung down from Pal's saddle, slipped and fell on my butt in the dust. But I was up again, with a wince, and digging in my medicine bag as I trotted over to a pair of wounded peasant men. A shallow slash on one man's arm had already clotted, so I only washed the wound and then held a cleansing charm over it.

The carved bit of wood held a knot of kir; with my mind, I picked the bound charm loose and its kir unfolded. Warm glow poured down onto the wound, calling up the man's own kir with its light. The injury had torn his kir's colorful whorls, but not badly. Once the wound was cleansed, I bandaged him. His older companion had a sprained elbow; I felt the joint to be sure it was no worse than that, and told him to drink some willow tea if it hurt so much.

By how he smirked, he'd only wanted an excuse to have my hands on him.

A shadow fell over us and the peasant startled, then dropped to one knee with his fist against his chest. I stepped back, myself, from the grey horse as it pranced close, mouthing its bit and puffing.

"I thought I told you to keep quiet."

I squinted up at the crown prince. I'd seen him at a distance, riding beside the king, and with my memory Blessing that was all I needed. Wodenberg had only one prince, and it was well known that the queen had sworn she'd die before she let the king touch her again.

A good thing that Prince Kiefan was so easy to look at, then, golden-haired and grey-eyed, Blessed as few were and still unwed at eighteen.

Stern glares were his stock in trade, it seemed. Like his father.

"These men were wounded," I said, then wanted to take it back as he towered over me. But then I steadied, sure that I was right. "How can I treat patients without speaking?"

M'lord leaned down from the saddle. "A squad of reinforcements doesn't need a physician at all, let alone a young girl. Keep quiet."

Fear stiffened my spine, kept my eyes on his black, shiny-new riding boot in the stirrup. "M'lord," I murmured, to accept the command. My mind whirled, though, flickering through Master Parselev's every word; he'd said I must go, Saint Qadeem had agreed, surely there could be no mistake...

The prince's horse still fidgeted, full of energy from the charge. Prince Kiefan tapped him and trotted off toward Sergeant Brauer and the growing cluster of Guard. "Fire's under control," the prince announced. "We're off."

I was quick to tie my medicine bag shut and climb back onto Pal as the party began to trot out of the little town. Tight muscles in my thighs protested, but with a hard heave and a boost on the rump from Ilya — bless him for not smirking — I was in the saddle.

CHAPTER 2

Some ways past Gabel, the prince whistled and turned his grey off the road. Pal followed the horses a few steps to stop near a well and a long trough dug into the ground. The stone walls lining the road made room for our party and even the two dozen Guard behind us. "Rest and water the horses," our leader commanded, easily swinging down from his saddle.

In a moment, I was the last one a-horse. Working one foot free, I picked myself up and swung but a muscle sharply protested, making me lose my balance and scrabble at the saddle as I fell. My ankle twisted in the stirrup and jammed before I landed. One leg in the air, I got up as far as my elbows before the pressure on my ankle stopped me.

I had my free foot down and was trying to lift myself with that and one hand, reaching for the stirrup, when boots came running.

"Father's beard, did you fall? Are you hurt?" Strong arms scooped me up and he hoisted me against his shoulders. He smelled of oiled mail and leather. "Wedged in there good," the knight said as I reached for my stirrup.

Pal shifted to back away and the knight clicked his tongue a few times. Pal's ears straightened and he stood still. My rescuer pried my boot free, thankfully, and I put both feet down.

"Thank you, sir…?"

He'd let his hood down and thrown his cloak's shoulders back; the open sun bleached his hair to palest blond and his eyes matched the sky. He'd been Blessed by Saint Woden — two ridges of grey horn erupted at his hairline and cut across his crown. Scar tissue hemmed the line between scalp and Blessing like a fingernail cuticle. Between the ridges, his knight's crest was long enough to tie in a flaxen pig tail but the rest was only grown back enough, since Ansehen, to color his scalp. All the knights shaved their heads down to a crest the eve before battle, and many kept that bit of a tail even if they never rode again.

His tabard had a sergeant's single brass ring knotted on each epaulette to mark his rank in the Prince's Guard. His sword, hanging from a double-wrapped belt, barely cleared the ground by his foot.

"Anders," he supplied. "Sir Anders Bockmann." He had an infectious smile, too. With a glance around at the empty road, the oat fields, and the mild commotion at the well, he sketched a bow. "Dame Kate, a pleasure to meet you even if you were upside-down at the time. Not broken?"

I checked. "Only a little twist." I'd skinned the heels of my hands, and brushed the dirt out of the scrapes.

"First time on a horse? Walk a bit." Anders gestured at the space around the well. "Stretch your legs before they knot up."

I had to agree. "They're sore already." My hood had slipped a bit and I pulled it back up as I took a few steps. My ankle hitched a little, but I kept going.

Anders walked with me. "Riding's more work than it looks."

"But easy enough for you, if you know horses so well. Or only Pal? That was a command, wasn't it, the…?" I clicked in imitation.

He nodded. "Hold," he translated. "Bockmann horses, all, to get us to Vorspitz." Turning, Sir Anders whistled short and sharp and some two dozen horses looked toward him, ears perked. But then the first bucket of well water was tipped into the trough and they jostled to drink.

I kept walking, circling the watering-stop. Prince Kiefan stood holding the well's rope as the massive bucket drained. He tracked us, a faint frown marring his brow. I pulled my hood further up, ears burning, and continued. He'd told me not to speak. Twice.

"You're limping a bit," Sir Anders said. "Are you sure it's not sprained? Here, I know a sprain from a break."

He indicated the field's stone wall and I leaned against it. Sir Anders had my boot and wool sock off in a moment and stroked both hands up my foot. My bones shifted a little, pinching the corner of my mouth. By how he checked my ankle, he did know a thing or two. And it might be a mild sprain but it was no break.

11

"No, I'm sure you're not a horse," he said, flashing me a grin.

I couldn't help a chuckle. His thumb massaging my instep was nice, too. "Checking my soundness?" I asked, quietly.

"Can't have you foundering—"

Sir Anders' head jerked hard as the prince appeared behind him; there must've been a cuff across the head, too quick to see. Then Sir Anders was eye to eye with the prince, both tensed and sharp, before I could gasp in surprise. Speed Blessings on both of them, and now that Sir Anders was half turned away I could see how his horn ridges joined and continued as one down the back of his head. They followed his spine down neck, betwixt shoulders, all the way to —

I couldn't see that part, of course, under his clothes. We'd had knights on the operating table often enough during the Ansehen battle that I'd seen most of their secrets. Admittedly, the thought of these two knights in less than full mail and winter cloaks made for a distracting thought.

Prince Kiefan spat something, and it took my Blessing a moment to recognize and point me toward the translation. It was Arceal, something to the effect of, "Keep your eye on the mission and not her."

Sir Anders bowed, curtly, and went to help see to the horses.

My pulse jittered as the prince spared me a glance. "Keep your hood up and quiet," was all he said.

I sat in my saddle, sweating under the felt, holding my tongue. Despite the strange, dramatic morning in the Grand Chapel and the harriers at Gabel, this day had turned stiflingly dull.

The road delivered us to the Felsherz River, which crossed the broad valley from the eastern Eispitzen mountains to join the Neva River. Clusters of a few houses around a tavern and an Orderhaus cropped up on the roadside every now and then. We kept riding even though people came out to see us. Cantered through, even.

Prince Kiefan let us rest often enough, but didn't speak or even wave when we passed vegetable wagons or knots of harvesters scything the fields. Sir Anders and Ther Boristan and Ilya handled that. They chattered along for hours about horses and riding gear, happy as magpies. The Prince's Guard rode at the rear, in orderly lines.

I kept quiet, as ordered.

Since Prince Kiefan had spoken some Arceal, I closed my eyes and reviewed my lessons in that language. Because Saint Qadeem Blessed me with memory at twelve, I could recall any moment of any day in perfect clarity. My horn ridges weren't so pronounced as a knight's speed or anticipation Blessing, but the two grey nubs at my hairline were easy to spot. The rest barely peeked through my hair.

The saints chose their disciples for their own reasons. Odd, true, for Saint Qadeem to choose a peasant girl, but I'd been duly sent up to the Order's main campus for two years of reading and writing lessons. Languages had come later, after Master Parselev plucked me from the ranks of memory-Blessed students and apprenticed me. Odder, that, and there'd been some feathers ruffled over it. The Elect chose from the ranks of other physicians' apprentices — advanced students of worthy skill. Not some Englic peasant who could barely read. But elect and saints were never wrong in their choices. Not to be questioned, in the end.

Maybe someday I could ask Saint Qadeem why, if I dared.

The sun was low and the lone mountain, Woden, cast its long shadow. No question who owned this broad valley; Woden stood alone. Its city, Wodenberg, lying on its southern flank, was only a smudge in the distance. The castle, perched on the low sub-peak, caught the afternoon light.

A good stretch past another village, we came to a cistern in the stream's bank. Prince Kiefan chose the trodden-flat apron around the cistern's trough for a campsite and both Ilya and Ther Boristan set to unpacking our saddlebags. The prince began drawing water for all the horses, as he had each time we'd stopped.

Sour he might be, but he didn't turn up his nose at labor.

I landed on my feet from the saddle but a twinge in my ankle still made me wince. Then I tried to walk and found my thighs and butt had fused into one solid knot. Or so it felt. On Sir Anders' advice, I'd hobbled around whenever I was off Pal, but now I was reduced to mincing my way to the campfire circle where Ther Boristan was setting up his firewood.

Trees lined the quick-running river. Ilya hobbled to and fro to bring armfuls of branches. He suffered as much as I from the day's ride but he declined help from any of the Guard. Ther Boristan arranged kindling under his careful stack of wood. Pinching his thumb and two fingers together, he reached down to let his hand hover just over the clump of dry grass he'd tented with twigs. I felt a little kir move, echoing from him as he focused. A glow rose to his fingertips and gathered into a twinkle of light. Snapping his fingers, he dropped the spark charm onto the kindling. The grass caught, flames chewed up the twigs merrily and the fire was soon crackling.

I stopped Ilya when he stood up with a wince after watching the fire start. "You'll be quicker if you let me unknot those cramps," I said. "And I know you're suffering too, Ther."

"Would you have kir for both of us?" Ther Boristan asked.

"I've made no charms today," Ilya said, extending his right hand as if to shake, "but I'm no physician. Take mine and use it for yourself. I'll manage as I am." He was charm-handed. A single nub of horn broke the skin on the back of his right hand, where he could give his kir to someone else if he did not use his day's worth.

"No, I'll have some willow bark once he boils water," I said.

"I'll drink it," Ilya said. "Truly, Dame Kate, I'll be well. I've ridden before, simply not often. More than the two of you, likely."

I gave in. "Thank you. Let me see to Ther Boristan first. May I?"

Boristan stood stiffly from the campfire. "What do you require, m'lady?"

It was something of a reach, but I slipped my hand under the collars of his layered cotes at the back of his neck. Then I called my kir and it welled up warm in my chest. It tingled down my arm as I sent it along, and its glow rose on my hand as it gathered. Answering, Ther Boristan's kir rose to the light from inside him. It spun in little whorls and ripples of color across his skin, visible despite his clothes thanks to my hand on him.

In living flesh, kir took shape and danced in slow, deliberate patterns. Meridians carried fresh kir to the dances and helped orchestrate. Where flesh broke, the pattern was interrupted. Where kir was pinched or knotted, the flesh felt pain without a wound.

I sent my kir down Ther Boristan's spine, his prime meridian, and my gaze went with it. His kir tangled and stumbled where the muscles were tense and overworked. With a little focus, I smoothed them out. Like combing out your hair, the tangles fought it but I loosened them till they came free. As the whorls unknotted, the muscles relaxed and the pain faded.

"Mustn't tell your wife of Dame Kate's studying your ass," Ilya said with a smirk.

I think Ther Boristan blushed, under his beard. "Is that why you declined?"

"She'd be angry if she learned." Ilya nodded. "Now for yourself," he said to me, holding out his hand again.

I laid my palm on Ilya's charm-node and kir tingled, tickled, through my skin and up my arm. Sending it down my spine, I combed it through my own knotted kir. It put up a bit of struggle and I had to go carefully, finding the larger tangles and twisting them loose. Little by little, they came free.

"Much better." I smiled. "Now, what can I do while the water boils?"

They sent me to unpack the bedrolls while Ther Boristan cooked for just the few of us. The Guards saw to their own, though I think they grew jealous as the mouth-watering scent developed. Ilya dutifully drank the bitter willow bark tea to ease his own aches the simpler way. The horses jostled around Sir Anders, as he had the feedbag of oats, and he spoke to them in clicks and whistles as he portioned out their dinners. When it came to our own meals, I was handed a trencher, a handsome wooden trencher, covered with pan-cooked potatoes and cabbage and salt pork. I started to pass it on, but the others already had theirs. It was all for me.

I was hungry enough to lick it clean. It was stunningly delicious. Ther Boristan only shrugged. "My wife lets me cook," he admitted. "That gives her more time to weave."

The sky darkened overhead as I helped clean up. Five of the Flock moons were high in the sky and a sixth was rising. The seventh, the shy one called Love, would not be back until the Shepherd waned. Puffy clouds caught the last light as the sun fell below the western mountains. When I crossed my legs by the stone-ringed campfire again, the shadows were thickening in earnest.

My bedroll tempted me. But something more important had stewed me all day. Prince Kiefan had told me to be quiet and I had.

None of this had been my plan, or anyone's other than my master and Saint Qadeem, but obeying had come easily enough. More than simply being the prince, he carried himself like an alerted tomcat. Both the knights did. Sir Anders could break that illusion with one of his easy grins, but on Prince Kiefan it only made me think of the stories I'd heard after the battle at Ansehen. Of the cavalry charge he'd led, and that on the battlefield his Blessings made him unstoppable.

"Majesty?" I had to know. "May I ask something?"

Across the fire, Prince Kiefan glanced at me. "You may. But 'Sir Kiefan,' not 'majesty.' Not out here."

"This can't be to deliver reinforcements, can it?" Once I started, I couldn't help saying it all. "Even if the prince went himself, he wouldn't bring a Ther and a physician's apprentice. And why leave before dawn, hoods pulled up and silent?"

I'd thought he'd glare or snap but he only watched, eyes measuring me. I'd let my braid down, for the night, and wrapped it around my hand as I waited. Sir Anders, sitting beside him, raised his eyebrows when the prince glanced at him sidelong.

Prince Kiefan — Sir — said, "Baron Eismann sent word that the lamia have been growing bolder of late. Coming down from the kir fount on Himmelbaum and taking sheep. Children, too. We're to lead a hunt of them before the snows get too deep and the lamia get any hungrier. Do you know about them?"

Monsters. They haunted the Winter Wood, in children's tales. "Only what stories say. Are they so dangerous as the monsters Arcea sent to invade us?"

"Centaurs are made things," Sir Kiefan said, "Saint Woden told us. Forged by Arcea's saints from men and horses. Lamia are animals — raised on the waters of a kir fount, but only animals. The kir makes them powerful. Clever."

When he paused, I asked, "As kir makes the Blessed powerful?"

"I've never hunted lamia. Baron Eismann wrote that a physician is prudent to bring. Lamia are cunning and cruel. He'll advise us as best he can." His voice dropped as his thoughts strayed, and it seemed he left much unsaid.

"But why must I hide? Why bring Ther Boristan? Surely they have Thers of their own."

16

He fixed me with a steady look and spoke slowly. "We meant to bring the Elect, but lacking him — this is no place for a girl that's not discipled to Saint Woden. So keep your hood up. We're hunting lamia. That is what you've been told."

My head cocked, on reflex, weighing that. There was more to come, I didn't doubt. "Yes, m'lord," I responded, quietly. "I see."

I thought I saw the corner of his mouth pick up a little, at that.

Ther Boristan rode with a book open in his hands, and I tapped Pal until he ambled up alongside. Ther sketched on the blank page with a piece of charcoal wrapped in linen. He noticed me and, with a smile, tipped it for me to see. It was Sir Kiefan, caught looking away and his Blessing's ridges rising fierce and sharp through the down of regrowing hair. His braided knight's crest swung as if he'd turned abruptly.

Leaning close, I whispered, "It's a good likeness."

Ther Boristan shrugged, humble. "Blessings fascinate me. Especially those few with multiple Blessings. To think we've two of them here — I couldn't help trying a sketch. I hope you don't mind if I sketch you? The memory Blessing's uncommon, too."

Fortunately, Sir Anders and the prince were absorbed in conversation, safely ahead of us. I could disobey a little. I murmured, "I wouldn't mind. What about your Blessing? Saint Qadeem spoke to you, I saw." Ther had nothing on his head, nor his hands, so I thought he must have the strength Blessing, which was easy to conceal. That was one of Saint Aleksandr's Blessings, though, as well as Saint Woden's. Not Saint Qadeem's at all.

Boristan offered his hand to me. "Craft-handed, m'lady. It barely shows. Both Saint Qadeem and Aleksandr have been kind to me."

I felt his fan of bones and knuckles -- oversized, true, now that I touched them -- and sure enough, the ridges lurked below his skin. "No surprise your sketch is so true, then."

Ilya slowed down on the other side, curious. He nodded when Ther Boristan showed him the sketch. "So serious," Ilya said, of it. "He does smile sometimes, truly."

"Does he?" Ther Boristan commented, for me.

17

"M'lord does smile. I've worked in the castle long enough to see it for myself. Heard a laugh, even. When His Majesty isn't on hand, the prince isn't much different from any other young knight. More serious, perhaps."

"His Majesty's serious indeed."

"He keeps Prince Kiefan close under his wing," Ilya said, his humor fading. But then he grinned again. "Many a maiden wishes he didn't, that's the Father's own truth. But he's a good prince. Never puts on airs, like some nobles do."

I kept to a murmur, leaning toward Ilya. "You work in the castle?"

"Oh, yes, always have. Since Papa let me tag along with him to the stables. Started me in the scullery and I picked up a bit here, a bit there. Whatever's needed around the courtyard, I'm your man."

"On hunting trips, too?"

Ilya nodded. "The hounds know me well. Nearly got myself gored by an elk, one hunt, up on Lake Neva. Majesty gave me a bonus for that, while I was laid up from the trampling. Very kind of him."

Boristan had gotten in a few more lines on his sketch, adding Kiefan's shoulder. "Have you been on hunting trips?" I asked him.

"Me? No, never. Since I took vows, I'm either home or at the Order. The abbot wants me on hand." When I nudged for more, he said, "I've been his secretary going on ten years now."

As I thought it, I said, "They must trust you."

"He's trusted me with private things, now and then. Things not to be spoken of."

A trustworthy servant and a trustworthy secretary. "Sir Anders must be worthy too."

Both men looked at Sir Anders' back when I said that, and hesitated. It was Ilya who said, "Sir Anders earned his place on the Prince's Guard at the jousting tournament. He rode beside m'lord at Ansehen, in the charge against the centaurs. In the saddle, true, he's a worthy knight."

"I saw enough of what they did to knights, in the surgery with Master Parselev," I said. As I thought of my teacher, I stumbled back across the question from that morning in the Chapel. "You expected the Elect to come with you."

Neither of them wanted to answer that. "I don't think anybody expected you," Boristan said. "A young girl like you? On a hunt? Folk would talk. No surprise he told you to keep quiet."

"I doubt it's a hunt." My voice dropped further. "Why did Sir Kiefan set a watch overnight? The Guard had their own watch, and surely that's enough. Do they set watches on hunts?"

Ilya answered. "To guard against wolves and bears. M'lord said it was to set the habit."

"Have you ever hunted lamia? Does one watch for them?"

"They're looking," Boristan murmured.

I glanced up, right into Sir Kiefan's eyes. A hot blush on my cheeks, I tugged on Pal's reins until he sidled away from Ther Boristan's horse.

I said nothing and let Pal trail a little behind the group until we stopped to eat at noon. Trail biscuit in hand, I walked while the horses drank from the trough at another cistern. Though today was better than yesterday, it was more an achy shuffle than a walk.

The valley spread out behind us, now clearly lower and gentler than the hills we'd been riding up and down all morning. Mount Woden still towered in the distance, its flanks dark with forest, its peak naked stone. On the road ahead of us, forested hills climbed fast and ascended into the cloudbank shrouding the Eispitzen mountains.

"Were you gossiping?" Sir Kiefan stood a few feet away, chewing on his trail biscuit as he watched me.

I was struck dumb for a heartbeat, under those chilly grey eyes. "Appreciating Ther Boristan's art, m'lord. Then Ilya told us about hunts."

A nod. "Ilya's served on several hunts with us."

"He said you set watches, on hunts, against wolves and bears."

The prince stepped closer. "True enough. And oat fields crawl with wolves and bears, as everyone knows."

"It did seem odd, m'lord."

"What does the Elect's apprentice know of setting watches?" he asked, drawing closer still. I looked away from his stern eyes, swallowing. The biscuit crumbled in my grip.

"How long have you been apprenticed?"

"Two years, m'lord."

"Where were you born?"

19

"In Wodenberg. On Engl Street."

I could smell horses and leather on him. A bit of sweat from hoisting buckets of water. The prince said, "Your parents are un-Blessed."

For that, I braved his eyes to be sure he saw my honesty. "My father and mother both swore to Saint Aleksandr, m'lord."

"And they raised a girl who won't keep quiet and keep her nose to herself."

"A timid physician is of little use, Master Parselev taught me."

A moment passed. I held my eyes on his, mostly. The scar tissue around the foremost nubs of his Blessing kept drawing me upward — silvery, raised spider-legs as if there'd been more that didn't quite surface. He took a step back. "We'll reach Vorspitz today. Can you hold your peace until tonight?"

"I'll burst for all my questions, m'lord," I replied.

Sir Kiefan was walking away, but he turned on his heel to say, "That would be curious to see, I think," and then kept going.

CHAPTER 3

The promise of answers helped me hold my peace through the day's ride and then dinner at Baron Eismann's own table in his keep's great hall. His wife and daughter served us themselves, with gracious smiles and no questions why I was counted among this hunting party. Little was said at all, in truth, until the Baroness took a steaming charger of apple strudel from a servant outside the hall and carried it to the table. I regretted eating so much of the venison pie, but was determined to have some of the strudel once the scent hit me.

"I've given you my two best huntsmen," Baron Eismann began, as he leaned on the table with both elbows. Sir Kiefan had declined to take the baron's seat at the head of his own table in his own hall, and Eismann had insisted that the prince sit at his right. "They've been as high as any man who's gone up Himmelbaum and Starknadel and lived to tell of it. Move quick, don't hunt, and the lamia may let you pass."

Bjorn and Ulf Waldgrun — cousins — had joined us for dinner and, after polite introductions, sat silently. Sir Kiefan had presented me as "his physician" and they'd given me a moment's measurement. From archers Blessed with hawk's eyes, that was something. Whatever color their eyes had been, they were golden now and crowded out the whites so their pupils could gape wide in dim light. Archers blinked rarely, letting a near-transparent inner eyelid do the job most often. Both were ten years and more my elder, Ulf seemingly sewn from grizzled leather by Father Duty's strong hands. Bjorn, the younger of them, smiled more but all about him was spare and sober.

Baron Eismann paused as his wife poured mugs of spiced, Arceal tea; I picked mine up as soon as she finished, wanting a taste of the exotic brew. Black tea was pricy enough, and Master Parselev rarely opened his box of spiced leaf.

"What knowledge can I give you as well, m'lord?" the baron asked.

"Do you see many Suevi in Vorspitz?" Sir Kiefan asked in reply. "Arceal merchants?"

It wasn't what Eismann expected, by how he frowned and stroked his grey-shot beard. "Here? It's a hard day's ride to Knapptal. And your grandfather saw to it that the pass is well watched, m'lord. How could Suevi reach Vorspitz?"

The Empire of Arcea had conquered Suevia, the land below Wodenberg's broad mountain valley, in the days when Kiefan's grandfather ruled. Arcea had been content to let Suevia and Wodenberg continue trading as neighbors for near fifty years. Then, over the summer, they'd sent an army of Suevi and kir-forged Arceal monsters to our southern border.

"Whatever smuggling there may be is of no consequence now," Sir Kiefan said, leaning toward the baron on one elbow. "The secrecy of this mission is of utmost importance. Must I watch my back all the way up the mountain? Through the pass? Arcea must not know we've tried for an alliance with Caercoed."

We were going through the Eispitzen? I'd caught a glimpse of the mountains in the afternoon, when the cloudbank lifted. Trees were barely turning for autumn here, but above was ice and snow. I managed to swallow the bit of strudel in my mouth, but suddenly didn't want any more.

Eismann, after leaning back and frowning, said, "There are a few Suevi who come this far. The King knows of them — they bring news from the Queen's kin. One brought a warning a week ago, and has already gone back."

"The word of their army massing at Temitte?" Kiefan grimaced. "Their harriers were bold enough to raid within an afternoon's ride of Mount Woden. Next year will be hard."

Temitte was the nearest Suevi city to our southern border.

I looked at the portion of strudel on my trencher, my stomach sinking under dread. The golden apples and pastry, cloaked in honey, glistened, trying to tempt me. While I considered one more bite, a warm head laid itself on my thigh. I sat at the end of the bench, and one of the baron's hunting hounds looked up at me with sad brown eyes. He licked his greying chops and stared longingly at my portion of strudel.

Across from me, Bjorn whispered, "Old Ritter's always glad to help, if you're full."

Tearing off a piece of the pastry, I gave it to Old Ritter and he hurried off. At the other end of the table, Sir Kiefan said, "Tell me what you know of the land beyond the mountains."

Eismann took another sip of his tea. "If any of us have reached Caercoed, they have not returned. Better to ask the Englic or the Suevi what they know of it." The baron's eyes fell squarely on me, the only Engl at the table.

"I was born in Wodenberg, m'lord," I said. "My father was never a sailor, nor any of his kin."

"A hunting party found the remains of a group lost years before," the baron went on. "They'd reached the far side of the pass and glimpsed a vast, green land. The archer saw smoke from villages in the distance. Then they were caught in a blizzard for days. Their food ran out as they struggled to cross back. Lamia finished them off, but did not touch the book the Ther had written in."

"A green land in winter?" Sir Anders broke his silence.

"The party went late in the Warm Moon."

Summer. Early, but full summer. Mother have mercy.

"The pass over Starknadel is the lowest in Wodenberg," Baron Eismann said, "but the snows never thaw. The pass is never easy — and the Grain Moon has begun in earnest. To be plain, m'lord, you should not go that way. South, over the smugglers' trails, then turn north in Suevia through one of their lower passes, and you might still beat the winter if you ride hard."

Kiefan hadn't eaten much of his strudel either, but the baron's daughter refilled his mug. Old Ritter laid his head on my thigh again, and let me scratch his soft ears.

"Whatever risk Starknadel offers, there's no chance of capture by Arcea," Kiefan replied. "No chance I'll be used as a hostage against my father."

"There's wisdom in that, m'lord, but sending you both?" The Baron included Sir Anders, on his left, with a glance.

Sir Anders? My brows crept together.

"The saints were clear. If there's to be an alliance, there's to be a marriage, and I am the heir. All they named to this party are here, in obedience. If the mountain keeps me, my eldest nephew has time to earn the job." That with a sidelong look.

"Your nephews are fine boys, m'lord, but we'd rather have you for king."

In the silence that followed, the wind rose and fell outside the baron's manor house. The heavy, split logs held without creaking, sound and warm. Far off, though, a clear high note lingered after the wind. Was it a woman's voice? A child's? A second joined it, a slightly lower note. Then a third, weaving up and down. A shiver tickled my spine.

The baron took no notice, nor did half the table. "They say it's a land of amazons," Sir Anders said.

Ther Boristan had stopped eating when the distant singing began. "Like Saint Woden's disciples?"

"In their own way. Twin saints rule there, twin women, and the men call cooking and diaper-changing a good day's work," Anders replied.

Boristan laughed, but hushed himself. "It must be a strange land. Where do the stories come from?"

"Merchants who've been to Temitte and seen traders from Caercoed. Strange, perhaps, but surely a land ruled by women could not be unpleasant."

"Their men must do more than cook, if they've held their southern passes against Arcea," Sir Kiefan said, and drained his tea again. "Hardly a day's work, changing diapers."

Anders chuckled. "Said by one who's never been handed a little sister to watch. I thanked the Father the day I was claimed for a stableboy."

Old Ritter whimpered, having been so patient, and I paid him with a bigger piece of strudel. The keening voices still rose and fell in the distance, drowned out by the occasional gust of wind. Ther Boristan finally asked, "Who could be out singing at night, m'lord?"

Baron Eismann seemed surprised. "That's the lamia, Ther."

I was given the smallest of the guest rooms as my own, and the men shared the others. My boots had hardly been off in two days, and when I sat on the mattress and unlaced them it took some two-handed wiggling to get them loose and then some peeling for the wool socks. The floor was chilly under bare feet, but no worse than my dormitory room at the Order. The baron's daughter had said she'd return with a hot water bladder for my bed.

I got up to shut my door. Glancing down the hall — I was at the end — I saw her, lamp in hand, leaning against the wall opposite Sir Anders. They spoke too quietly to hear, but she laughed at something he said and played at sassing back with one fist on her generous hip. He laughed in return.

Anders shifted to put his hand to the wall beside her and lean on it. She turned her nose away, haughty, but spoiled the effect with a smile. He caught her chin with two fingers and turned her back for a kiss.

I felt a blush rise on my face. I pushed the door shut but couldn't help lingering with one eye at the shrinking crack.

The baron's daughter stepped around him and he turned, leaned against the wall where she'd been. She took a few steps, looked back, and then kept walking. After a few moments, Sir Anders followed.

I never did get that hot water bladder.

I slept in my woolen cote and tried to pretend it was a proper shift but it barely reached the middle of my thighs. My feet were cold all night. Next morning, it was back into the rest of the boy clothes. The too-big hose still sagged and the garters for my wool stockings at home would've fixed that but no, men had to do things their own way. Run them all the way to your waist and lace them together with your braies — or, I had found out, men could string them separately so they didn't drop everything when they only needed to pee.

The things you learn on the road.

25

Not being built for that sort of convenience, I assembled a clean set of clothes while sitting on the straw mattress and dressed. I pulled the heavier, looser surcote on over my cote, fussing with the long sleeves to get them all evenly settled together. There'd been time before dinner, thankfully, for me to comb out my hair and re-braid it. Wrapping the braid around my head again, I picked up my wooden hairpin and secured braid to braid at the base of my skull.

The baroness fed us as much breakfast as we would eat. The seven of us — now that we had two woodsmen and left behind the Prince's Guard to reinforce the baron's soldiers — sat around the kitchen table and cleaned out bowls of oatmeal, apples, fried potatoes, eggs, whatever she gave us. Old Ritter wanted to know if I needed help. I didn't.

M'lady was so kind in calling me Physician Carpenter and overlooking my table manners that my throat choked shut when she slipped me a packet of horehound lozenges. The Baroness smiled at my thanks and promised to pray the Mother watch over us.

Afterwards, there was last-minute packing to see to — fresh provisions from the kitchen, and new gear that Bjorn and Ulf brought. Instead of our horses, we met two shaggy ponies in front of the stables. The larger of them, Acorn, could look me in the eye if he held his head high enough. Puck didn't care to try. The stable master caught Sir Anders checking the ponies' hooves and took offense, setting off an argument until Baron Eismann and Sir Kiefan arrived to break it up.

Bjorn managed the packing of the baggage and the messenger bags he handed out. I already had the medicine bag that Master Parselev had given me, though I'd hardly used it yet. Bjorn gave me a couple trail biscuits tied in a kerchief to keep with the bandages and charms — "For emergencies," he said — and a small water skin on a baldric. The little eating knife on my belt was not sufficient, apparently, and he changed it for a double-edged blade as long as my hand.

"What could I do with a dagger?" I asked. Aside from slice myself open.

"You never know what you'll need," Bjorn said.

There were thrummed mittens and wool gloves and a snug cap to be packed in my bag, too. Overnight, the maids had stitched fur linings into our hoods and our cloaks. They gave me three extra cloak pins. There had been a hint of frost before the sun rose, but it wasn't cold enough to endure the sunshine. Not cold enough for all this new gear, or for the heavy blanket rolls the men added to the ponies' loads on top of coils of rope and oilskin tarps, the cuts of smoked meat and sacks of oats. There was some debate over how much the ponies would need and how much we'd eat. And how long we'd be out there.

Sir Kiefan and Anders had traded their mail suits for lighter, boiled-leather breastplates worn over their surcotes. We had swords and bows, spare quivers and daggers, shovels and an iron-bound pry-bar that could bash a man's head in.

We were ready for trouble in the unknown. Expecting it, maybe. Beyond the baron's stockaded keep, the Eispitzen were free of clouds for now. Though the sun rose behind them, their brilliant white snow carried the morning light. Forests ascended from below, black in the mountains' shadow, but the trees couldn't climb far against the creeping blanket of winter that lived on the slopes and descended every year.

And the saints had sent us to cross through it.

———————✝———————

"You won't be saddle-sore tonight," Sir Anders said, catching up to me after a short trip behind a tree. The road was one wagon wide and the cleared shoulders only a few feet more than that, so it was a quick diversion even with a pony trailing him. Anders led Puck, who had declined to have his reins tied to Acorn so Ilya could lead both ponies.

"No, but this is nearly as steep as River Road."

And had been all morning. We walked in half-shade under trees dotted with yellow leaves, the first thoughts of autumn. I had slowly fallen near the back of our party, but Ulf still brought up the rear. Or so I thought; he was only there half the times that I looked. Neither woodsman seemed worried, as yet, so the lamia could not be close by. The Felsherz ran quick and foamy from pool to pool and each had a clot of fishers' cottages on its shores. Shepherds' folds, too. We were not so deep in the forest, yet.

"You and Elect Parselev were at the quartermaster's pavilion the evening we laid camp at Ansehen, weren't you?"

I blinked, pulled from my musings. On cue, that memory passed through my mind. "Yes. An extra wagon of hay and oats turned up at the infirmary instead of our sleeping tents. Master wanted to show me the proper channels to go through with the quartermaster's staff."

He chuckled, at that. "So you got my missing feed."

"Your missing feed?"

"I'm master of the horse for the Prince's Guard," Anders said. "I was there about a wagon of hay and oats as well. A shame we didn't happen to meet then, we could have cleared it up quickly."

It had been a chaotic pavilion, or seemed so to me, all managed under the hawk's eyes of the duchess of Prohzgrad. To find Sir Anders in it, I had to comb through a still moment of my memory to find him. I hadn't noticed one more mail-clad knight in a black tabard, even if it did have two gold stars on it for the Prince's Guard.

"You saw me there?" I asked. "In all that confusion?"

He infected me with another one of his smiles. "I always notice a pretty face. Even in a crowded room."

There wasn't much to say to that, so I said, "I only caught a couple glimpses of you. Duchess Vysokova was in a dark mood, by all the shouting."

"M'lady was not pleased by how many things had gone wrong. I saw you beside the Elect and thought you must be that apprentice there's been a fuss about. Prettier than I expected."

"What did you expect?" What had 'pretty' to do with apprentices?

"Perhaps I didn't expect, exactly. The fuss I'd heard had been over older students being passed by in favor of some Englic peasant girl." Sir Anders took on a stuffy, disgruntled voice as he went. "Outrageous. A fourteen-year-old peasant? Chosen by the elect when she can barely read?"

I couldn't help a grimace. "I read well enough. I studied hard, those two years."

"I don't doubt it," Sir Anders said. "If they'd known you were pretty to boot, they'd have been doubly outraged. There." He tucked a black-eyed susan under my braid, just by my ear. As I'd been glaring at the pebbly dirt road, I didn't see the bright yellow coming and flinched at first.

My father and mother had told me I was pretty, now and then. It rarely came up when there was so much studying to do and so many patients to see to.

"I saw you after the battle," Sir Anders said, voice a little lower now that he walked closer by me. "A friend was in the infirmary with a gash in his side, and I tracked him to there. You were trying to feed one of the worse-off men. Barely conscious and twitching, but you kept trying to get some soup into him. I thought it a touching scene. Compassionate."

He looked me in the eye and it sounded likely enough. Except... "After the battle? That afternoon?"

A moment's thought. "I believe so. I hauled Viktor out of there and was back in time for dinner. Late afternoon."

I had to say, "I was in the surgery with Master Parselev until full dark. That wasn't me you saw."

His turn to echo. "In the surgery?"

"There was a late ambulance of knights from the king's attack."

"Are you sure? She wore her hair braided up, like you."

"You don't think I misremember, do you?" I tipped my head toward him an inch or two. He was tall enough that he ought to have a good view of my Blessing in any case.

That quieted him. There were several women with blonde hair long enough to braid and wrap. I usually let my braid hang free, as I wasn't wed yet. "It's not so odd to confuse me with one of the Ters," I said, to excuse him in an honest mistake.

Anders frowned, and then a burst of open sun made him squint as well. When we reached a patch of shade, he looked over at me. "Still, I was glad to see you again at the chapel that morning. A touch of kindness will do the journey well."

That late ambulance had been full of broken bones on men who'd survived lying or crawling for hours on the field. As we'd been out of charms, and kir, and even my master exhausted by then, it had been a great deal of blood and screaming. The saw and the cauterizing iron had been needed. Little kindness to speak of, at a glance.

"If you'd fallen from your horse and come to me with both leg bones jutting from your flesh, you might think differently."

Sir Anders said nothing after that, and I let my pace slow as my ankles were aching. He didn't seem to notice, and then a whistle from up ahead marked that we were stopping to rest. A small branch in the road led down to the Felsherz.

As Puck walked by, he reached with his lips and plucked my black-eyed susan to eat. I chuckled under my breath. A far better use for the poor flower.

———————————✝——————————

Evening light clung to the mountain peaks well after darkness fell on our camp. Their glowing slopes peeked through the high canopy when the lodgepole pines swayed in the high-up wind of winter drawing breath. I sat on a tarp eating ham pan-fried with cabbage and onions, stuffed into half a round of bread. The grease, soaked into the crust, kept me from stopping until it was gone. Ther Boristan, across the fire from me, wrote and sketched in his book. I'd volunteered to clean up after dinner so he would have time. Ilya brought the ponies back from their drink at the stream.

The song began with one note, again, high and pure and far more human than any monster had a right to sound. Two more voices joined in, then a third.

We all looked up, breath billowing before our faces, the quiet chat about horses between Sir Anders and Bjorn dropping.

"They're higher up, near the kir fount," Ulf said, after listening to the song. "Not likely to stalk us tonight, but we should set a watch all the same, m'lord."

"For wolves and bears?" Ilya asked.

Ulf shook his head. "Lamia drive out wolves and bears. They'll brook no competition in their forest from animals. Or humans."

CHAPTER 4

Saint-day began with frost. We'd slept atop one tarp and under another, each wrapped in a bedroll and laid alongside each other like sausages. As I had no watch duty, by morning I was in the middle of the sausage-line and had to crawl out on all fours when I woke. Ilya always drew the last watch and always began by stoking up the fire and checking the oats left cooking overnight in a spider-legged pot over the coals. When I saw him busy, I knew it was close enough to morning to get up.

Sir Anders settled beside me when the porridge was ready and passed me the maple syrup bottle with a smile. I added a dollop and passed it on to Ulf.

"You wake early," Anders said, between spoonfuls of oatmeal. "You left half of me cold when you climbed out."

"Was that you?" We all looked about the same when wrapped up. "You were up soon enough after me."

"Chills keep me awake — they get into my bones and then I'll be sore all morning. I wasn't going to get any more sleep, so I had to follow before the cold crept in." He even added a melancholy sigh.

Master Parselev had a keen eye for the health of anyone standing before him; he said it was a sense I'd learn with time. I couldn't claim to have too much yet, but Sir Anders wasn't ill-fed or consumptive. "Do you want me to believe you're so fragile? The master of horse for the Prince's Guard?"

That got me a wry smirk, so I guessed I'd scored a hit.

Then there was the cleaning up and the repacking to see to and we were underway by the time sun peeked into the forest. Our woodsmen knew a good place to set the next camp, they said, atop a water-

31

fall where there'd be a clear view of the valley. And we'd get there by noon, in time for the Saint-day washing and the disciple's dance.

"If we keep a good pace, we'll be there with time to spare," Ulf said. "And it's far enough from the kir fount that we won't draw the lamia."

We parted from the road — more a trail, in truth, since we'd passed through a tiny village yesterday — and climbed a slope that gave way to bald rock near the top. The Felsherz tumbled a few dozen feet onto rocks; at the top, it lay in a flat pool. Shorter, denser evergreens had replaced the lodgepole pines over the morning's walk and from here we saw just over their heads. The sun above was warm, once I was in it, and I pulled my hood back.

Hills fell away into golden prairie, and far in the distance the western mountains rose jagged and grey. Through the middle of the basin, the Neva River twisted southward toward its falls on Wodenberg's southern border. Mount Woden stood alone by the river. Its peak cut through the belly of a foolish puff of cloud as it passed over. That was one of a flock of clouds rolling eastward toward us, still some distance off.

"Weather changes quickly up here," Bjorn reminded us. "Clear one moment, ice or snow the next. And the river's fed by snowfields — ice cold, so take care. It'll nip you to buds, in washing, and kill you if you fall in."

I braved the pool first, bathing by halves. Men's clothes were good for that, I had to allow. In a dress, I'd have to strip entirely. Each of the men took a turn behind the hanging blanket at the shore, and we all went shivering to the fire to warm. Once Ther Boristan had the stew simmering, he went to wash last. In returning, he began the gathering song, which drew Sir Anders back from the ponies and the woodsman from hanging the tarp.

Ther Boristan took a moment to compose himself, and said, "I don't often give the homily, so I'll be brief. Saint-day so far from home is strange for most of us. Though we met only a few days past, we are as much a community of disciples as in our own Orderhäuser. We are answering the call of Father Duty and we've traveled under his protection thus far. Mother Love has kept the weather fair and the road clear for us." With a glance over his shoulder at the clouds, he added, "Pray she keeps it as fair as she can. Even though we're far from home, we will obey the instructions of those children the Father and the Mother sent to guide us: our saints. Saint Qadeem bids us wash, Saint Aleksandr bids us eat as a community, and Saint Woden bids us dance."

It took a moment for us to get all boots and socks off, and spread out around the fire. Boristan checked the stew.

Ther began with slow, careful stretches, held long to loosen our joints. Gently, at first. Then the poses progressed into deeper muscles, required more flexibility. Boristan did not push us so hard as some Thers; I could manage these, at least in part. And sidelong, I tracked the others. My eyes kept creeping to Sir Kiefan.

From stretching we moved into balance and focus, where I often wobbled and had to settle for the less intense poses. Ilya was with me in that, I was secretly glad to find. Ulf and Bjorn had all the focus of hunting hawks, and stood firm when even Ther Boristan and the knights began to waver.

Came the strength movement, which Kiefan and Sir Anders took with ease, and my legs were already crying for rest. Perhaps Boristan's were as well, for he eased up at last and didn't lead us to some of the toughest strength poses. I was sweating and breathing in time with my pulse when we finally stood, on both feet with palms pressed together, at the end.

"Thank you," Ther Boristan said with a bow. "Don't stray far. I'll call when the stew is ready."

I cast about for some chore to do, and thought of the work my master had given me for the journey. Ulf and Bjorn caught my eye, though, odd in their caution approaching me.

"Dame Kate," Ulf said, "you're the Elect's apprentice? And were at Ansehen?" When I nodded to both, the elder archer continued. "It's said the Elect stole Margrave Schutze back from the Shepherd. Did you see that?"

"The margrave was not dead." I was quick to correct him. "It was a mortal wound, yes, but the Shepherd didn't have him yet."

This drew Ilya, and Ther Boristan left off stirring the stew to listen. Sir Kiefan and Anders hesitated on the verge of starting sword drills a few yards from the campfire. "Tell us of it?" Ilya asked. "I heard it said, too, that the margrave died on the field. Or so most thought, until he walked into the command pavilion."

"He was in Vorspitz half a moon ago, but wouldn't speak of it," Bjorn said. "I told Johanna he couldn't have been dead — the Shepherd can't be cheated — but none of our garrison were at Ansehen. Please, m'lady?"

I settled by the campfire, cross-legged, and called up the memory to give them the truth.

Master Parselev's surgery, at Ansehen, was sectioned off from the main infirmary by canvas walls. We had kettles boiling just outside, for cleansed water, and cauterizing irons in the fire. The day had run long, already, through a stream of ambulance wagons bringing dozens of wounded from the battlefield. We stood catching our breath betwixt arrivals, drinking cups of water and washing what we could. In the general noise, I didn't hear more hooves riding up to the infirmary pavilion.

One Ther and a knight burst through the tent flap, carrying a travesty between them. My cup hand was suddenly empty and my shoes wet. They had the patient by a shoulder and knee apiece and I had no idea who he was. I could only see the length of four-inch sapling stake rammed through his ribs.

"No help for the dead!" Parselev shouted over their voices, putting up a hand.

"M'lord, please! He lives!" The knight — a lieutenant, by the brass rings on his epaulettes — heaved his burden onto the surgery table. "He's my lord, sir, please! Margrave Schutze!" The stake's sharpened end scraped on the table and its movement tore a weak cry from the man. The margrave. They rolled him on his side, the Ther putting a hand on the bloody end of the stake to hold it steady.

My master touched the patient, calling up his kir. His mouth pursed, tight. To the lieutenant, "You. Your day's kir?"

He blinked. "I have much of it. If you need it, take it." He held out his hand.

Only the charm-handed could give their kir, or so I thought. But Master Parselev gave him a sharp look and even I could feel the force he sucked the kir out with. It arced from the knight's hand to my master's chest in a golden strand. The lieutenant's knees buckled and I ducked under his arm to steady him. He dropped to his knees, gasping for breath. His tabard was soaked in blood; wetness seeped into my dress.

"Hold him," Master told the Ther who'd helped carry Schutze in. My master put his hand on the margrave and looked to Ter Biya, who aided him in surgery. She had a strength Blessing. "Biya, pull the stake. And Kate? Don't look away."

The margrave was ashy grey, barely breathing. Biya put both hands on the cruel stake and checked it with a little twist. Then she bit her lip, pulled with her Blessing strength, and it slid out red, ragged, scraping on bone. Gore splattered. Screams ripped out too, but they were sucked down into silence as kir blossomed in my master's hand, spinning up from his palm in knots of green and gold. I could feel it flowing through him, it was so clear and strong. The kir twisted, tightening down, stars igniting in the misty stuff until the whole mass of it lit with a flash, brilliant as the sun. Stars spun around the sun in my master's hand and scattered, confused, when he threw the mass of kir into the margrave's chest.

It landed on him in heavy ripples, like a cloak, and his body clenched. Kir patterns flooded the wound, pulling the flesh with them. The stars chased after, each strike sending out ripples of green and smoothing the kir's dance.

The world released the breath it held.

I wobbled at the suddenness, and my hand fell on the lieutenant's sweaty hair. He glanced up, startled, and hastily let go of my waist. I hadn't noticed him clutching me, either. He left me half covered in blood from his tabard. The Ther fell to his knees, letting the margrave drop onto his back. Biya already sat on the grass, the stake in her hands, her eyes calmly closed.

Master Parselev and I alone stood, in the room. Margrave Schutze breathed, unconscious, as the Ther straightened him on the table. Through the hole in his armor and gambeson, a purple bruise on the mended flesh roiled to a stop before my eyes.

"That lesson must wait, I'm afraid," my master told me with a thin smile. "Let's hope the king isn't brought in as well. A cup of water, please, Biya? Ther, take the patient out to a pallet. Lieutenant? You served your lord well today. I'll tell him that myself."

The lieutenant bowed, still on his knees. "Elect, I…"

"Stay with him now. He may wake before dark."

Scrambling to his feet, the lieutenant followed the Ther and his lord. Parselev took a fresh cup that Biya offered him and drank deeply as another Ther carried in the next wounded knight.

———————————————

My story earned me thanks and a few questions, but after that my audience melted away to their chores, scouting, and sword drills. It left me with little to do, so I hunted through my bags on Puck's back and dug out the book Master Parselev had entrusted to me. I hadn't known why, when I was packing, but now it was clearer. It was a philosophy text that I was partway through already. As it was written in Arceal, it was a struggle for me to work through the language. Arceal was a strange, jumbly tongue, not like Alemannic or the Englic I spoke at home with my parents.

I hadn't known how I could manage to read any more without my teacher. Now I had two knights on hand who had to know some Arceal. And if this Caercoed kingdom sent merchants to Temitte, they must speak Arceal themselves. I had both a reason to keep learning and the means, if I could find a way to ask one for help. Perhaps Sir Anders, if he could be weaned off the teasing and the flowers.

I settled cross-legged by the fire again to read.

A few words in, the crash of steel in the forest caught my ear. Both knights dashed into the campsite clearing, Anders leading by a few steps and pivoting into the prince's unprepared guard. My eyes could hardly catch Kiefan's block and counter-stab and Anders' tumble to one side that came up on his feet and ready as if he'd planned the whole thing.

They were far enough off that I only heard a mutter of what they said. By mutual agreement, they paused a moment to catch their breath and then started a new line of practice. Slow, at first, like the disciple's dance, swinging and blocking with the flats of their swords. When the pattern began again, they moved to half speed.

At full speed, I found I followed it clearly and could pick out the individual poses even as they blended together. But then they shifted into Blessing speed and it all became a frightening, blurry tangle that kept going far too long for the one series of moves. With a louder crash, one of them fell and they were on the ground scattering dry pine needles until they abruptly froze. Anders pinned Kiefan, a knee on his chest, arm drawn up to hold the sword-tip to the prince's throat.

I'd forgotten to breathe.

Sir Kiefan heaved up and threw Anders off like a blanket, proof of his strength Blessing. The prince brushed needles from his woolens, apparently unconcerned.

"The king should let you compete in the joust," Sir Anders said, on the edge of my hearing. "It would make for a more challenging tournament."

"We can't have any accidents."

Anders laughed. "But if it's a fool's quest across the Eispitzen, you're first in line."

Kiefan shot him a look. "Call the saints fools at your peril."

Anders seemed less than worried. Sheathing his sword, he went to his water skin for a drink. I'd forgotten all about my book in watching the duel, I realized, and searched for my place on the page.

"You brought a book?"

My finger on my place, I glanced up as Sir Kiefan crouched beside me. "Master Parselev wanted me to finish it. The dialogues about logic, if nothing else. It's to help me learn Arceal as well."

He leaned to look, braided knight's crest hanging free. "May I?" he asked, and took the book from me. Keeping a finger on my page, he checked through it. "Oh, I remember this. d'Ovio Alain, isn't it? I read 'On fear and love' from this. Father didn't give me time for any of the other dialogues."

"I'm partly through 'On proof' and I'm to read 'On reason and clarity' as well. Master Parselev didn't mention 'On fear and love.'"

"It's about ruling. Whether a ruler should strive to be loved or feared. I don't suppose a physician would have much need of that. Unless one should fear one's physician." Sir Kiefan said that with a smile as he handed the book back. Ilya was right; he did smile sometimes.

37

It nearly distracted me from replying. "No, love is far better for physicians. Trust. Honesty."

"Ah, honesty." Kiefan settled cross-legged beside me. "To be honest, I wanted to read 'On reason and clarity.'"

"To be honest, I'll be too slow in getting through it."

He considered. "I've spoken Arceal a bit. Perhaps I could help?"

Our eyes met and my mind was struck dumb by the thought of being tutored by the prince of Wodenberg. "I'm sure you could," I managed to say.

"Though I've never had reason to teach anything. Haven't had time for a squire, even."

I bowed my head. "Your honesty is appreciated."

"Well, you are my physician now," he said, and then pressed his mouth shut as if he hadn't expected that.

It hit me, too, that I was sole physician to half a dozen strangers now. "I should've asked Master Parselev for your history," came out of my mouth unbidden.

"He didn't tell you about the headaches, then," he said, his voice dropping to near a mutter.

A snowflake landed on the open book. Fat, slow flakes tumbled down, swirling when a breeze wandered by. Boristan, at the fire, said, "They didn't jest. I didn't smell snow coming."

I closed the book, asking Sir Kiefan, "You have headaches?"

He was looking up at the snow, but he nodded as he stood. "Ilya, we'll need to shelter the fire. Where's Bjorn and Ulf?"

"Just gone to look about, m'lord."

Then Kiefan was helping Ilya unpack another tarp for our shelter and I noted the headaches to ask him about later. Bjorn and Ulf came hallooing through the thickening snow soon after. They'd seen proof of lamia, both nearby and only a few days old.

CHAPTER 5

Snow still fell when Ilya shook me awake in the middle of the night. The patter of flakes on the overhead tarp blended with anxious whispers and sharp coughs. A pony puffed nearby and hooves shifted.

"Ulf says stay close," Ilya whispered in my ear. "Get the bedroll off and flat so nobody trips. Careful of Acorn, he's right here."

I blinked and rubbed at my eyes and a whiskery horse nose nudged my cheek. Acorn shifted away as I struggled out of my bedroll and to my feet. I put my arm over his neck for balance as I kicked the heavy blanket off and tried to spread it flat. Puck snorted, close by too.

The fire, half sheltered by our tarp lean-to, had lowered to glowing coals. Ulf and Sir Kiefan stood on the far side with their backs to it, one with bow and nocked arrow, the other with sword in hand. Kiefan asked something of the woodsman and he muttered a reply. Beyond them, the black forest waited, crusted by a layer of snow that glowed blue when moonlight fought through thin patches of the clouds. Tumbling flakes kept up a quiet patter as we all fell silent, even the ponies.

Fear drove off the lethargy of waking so late, but there was nothing to see in the clusters of squat pine trees and thickets. Ulf and Kiefan moved a few steps apart, tense and alert. I wanted to ask what was wrong.

Lantern eyes lit up beyond the fire, paced by, and vanished. A shape moved across a snow-laden pine branch. That coughing sound came again, from the moving shadow, and it was answered from behind me.

Ilya, holding Acorn's bridle beside me, whispered, "Mother Love, we're surrounded."

I sidled closer to the middle of the tarp, though it meant letting go of the solid mass of the pony. Ther Boristan stood holding Puck. A few steps out from that side of the lean-to, Bjorn faced the forest with bow and arrow ready. Beyond him, another pair of eyes caught the light.

"I could stoke up the fire," Ilya raised his voice to a murmur.

Ulf answered, as he was closest. "They're not afraid of fire. Whatever you do, stay together. Stand and fight."

I looked over Puck's rump, and Sir Anders stood watch on that last side with his sword in hand. A snow-covered bush there offered a clear backdrop for the form that stalked across it. The lamia were perhaps the size of a hunting hound, if bulkier in the shoulders. Their tails ran long and hairless, and lashed like a cat's.

I felt around in the dark mass of bedrolls and found my medicine bag. With it on, I was a little more useful. I'd taken my dagger off for the night, but I'd be little help with it.

A bit of wind drove the snowflakes in my face for a moment, then they fell back. The lamia stalked their circle around our smaller circle and coughed to each other in little patterns. Snow slowed its pace, and the moonlight strengthened. I watched along with Ulf and Ilya and Acorn, all of us shifting on our feet.

The lamia went still and silent. Ulf's bow rose as he drew his arrow halfway.

Snarling, a lamia charged from the trees. One long bound and the shadow split into two, one diving across Ulf's sights and drawing his bow, the other angling straight on into Anders. Puck shimmied back with a whinny, yanking Boristan off his feet. A second bound and the lamia threw itself under one blur of steel but the second blur as Anders twirled Blessing-fast caught the beast low in the spine. It screamed, far too human. Puck and Acorn wove and fought to get free, and someone's rump knocked me down. Hooves stomped all around me; I scurried under a pony's belly, only to stop short when movement on the snow yanked my eyes up. Four paws broke the white as the lamia angled toward me, the vulnerable one on the ground, and fangs caught the moonlight a moment before an arrow took the monster in the neck. It crashed from a full run.

Then, nothing. The ponies snorted and stamped, but after a few low whistles and clicks from Sir Anders they settled. Snowflakes kept pattering, definitely slower now. We waited.

In the distance, though not so far as I'd like, a lamia sang. A second joined it, cycling from louder to softer and back. Further away, a third note answered.

Ulf and Bjorn returned their arrows to their quivers. "They're done, m'lord," Ulf told Sir Kiefan. "They're reporting in to their lords."

"They won't return?" Kiefan returned to the fire, sword lower.

"Not tonight."

He surveyed the forest again. "They were testing our strength."

Ulf nodded. "They know what bows are, and they'll remember who has one."

"We killed two. Will that weaken them?"

"They hunt and lair in small groups, but there's always some master in the distance answering songs."

Sir Anders kicked the one he'd killed and lifted a paw with the point of his sword. "Any chance we'll get back to sleep?"

Bjorn laughed. "It takes cool blood to sleep after that. You're entitled to keep its teeth, since you killed it. They bring luck."

"Have you seen the kir fount on Mount Woden?" I asked Boristan as we walked through the mist. Last night's snow had melted quickly, but the vapors lingered around our ankles.

"Nobody goes to the fount itself but the saints," he answered. "It's near the peak. But I've been near enough to the Pool, with the abbot, to feel its kir. Through stone walls, it's so strong."

Soon after we packed up camp and set out, I'd felt a faint tingle over my heart. As we followed the shrinking Felsherz up, it strengthened. Even though I was tired after lying awake most of the night, the draw of the kir kept my feet moving. "Stronger than this?"

"You can feel it already?"

I looked back at him, surprised. "You can't?"

Boristan smiled. "You must be sensitive, m'lady." As we trudged on, he added, "As Master Parselev chose you for an apprentice, that should be no surprise."

We'd been put in the middle of the party, along with Ilya and both the ponies, so that a woodsman and a knight could guard us ahead and behind. The only noises in the forest were birdcalls and snow sliding off pine boughs.

The two dead lamia had been strange even in daylight. They were wolves raised on the kir-rich waters of the fount, Ulf had said. Their skulls had lengthened, their skin thickened to leathery hide over their hindquarters and their rat-tails grew long. The remaining fur on their forequarters was harsh, and a spiny crest rose between their shoulder blades. Even slack and dead, something about their eyes and face recalled a human's. There was a structure to it, a hint of cheekbones, despite the lupine muzzle and the fangs.

A few blows with the pry-bar and the menfolk had pulled out all of the monsters' fangs as prizes. Bjorn had shown me the distinct serrations that distinguished lamia's teeth from wolves'. Fakes were common enough, he'd said.

We followed the trail around tangles of rock and tree trunks that avalanches brought down during the winter. Young pines sprang up eagerly in the path of a slide, but even the older trees were small now. Brambles grew thick and close to the path, catching on my felt cloak. Topping one last rise, we clustered for a moment within view of a reed-lined pond. The stream, all that was left of the Felsherz, gushed out of it and down the slope. A heron took off from the cattails, heavy grey-blue wings thumping as it rose.

Ulf held up an arm and turned to remind us, "Stay together. The fount's just off the north side."

I could have told him that by how it tugged at me. The trees on the north side grew taller, thicker, and as the trail led us up I could see how they'd twisted in growing. Not content with that, they'd also coiled over as if bending to drink from the fount.

Puck's head was up, ears forward, and he actually hurried ahead as we approached. "Now I feel it," Boristan said, perking up himself. "Just a little fount, but it's still kir."

The near-human shriek from my left paralyzed me and the reeds on my right exploded. Puck shrilled and knocked me to the muddy ground as he bolted. Boristan stumbled and a black mass of crest and fangs and whipping tail tackled him. My feet scrabbled and I lunged up, off balance and blank-minded. The lamia's snarl sounded just behind me, far louder than any shouts. I ran, blind. The monster galloped after me, roaring, and it landed on my back like a falling wagon. Crusty snow in my face, blood in my mouth, a thousand pounds of snarling heat pinning me down.

A crash and a yell and the lamia landed on its shoulder beside me. Instantly, it was up and lunging and I was scrambling to my feet again. Growling and screaming — the scream human for sure. I swung around to see the lamia shake Bjorn hard and rip a mouthful from his bicep. Blood, a kir fount of its own. The gushing scarlet etched on my eyes clear as day. I kept running.

Trees scratched at me as I careened through them. Three lunging steps and I glimpsed the lamia, this time, looked it right in its leaf-green eyes as it tackled me. I screamed. Its hot breath, stinking of carrion, and the teeth —

Light flashed on metal and the hideous head fell on me, spasming and drooling. Its hot blood splashed my scrunched-tight face. A hand grabbed my arm and pulled me from under the beast's dead weight. I hit my rescuer's warm side, threw my arms around his waist and clutched. His arm wrapped across my shoulders. His chest pumped, breathing hard, and he twisted in my grip, shifting his crouch, to look for more trouble.

My face was against his cloak; I wiped my eyes clear on it. His sword drew a straight, bright line across the jumbled mass of autumn-gold shrubs around us. His breathing slowed. Kiefan spared a glance at me. "Hurt?"

I shook my head. He stood, bringing me along by the shoulders, and let his sword drop to a lower guard. I found my feet and his arm loosened.

In the distance, a shout. "M'lord?"

"Here!" he called back, turning toward the pond.

"Bjorn," I breathed, remembering; breaking loose, I pushed past a young pine and cast about. "Bjorn?" I called. Silence. Past a second tree, I found the blood — sprayed droplets on golden leaves, a long stain on the ground. Bjorn's bow lay nearby, and a few loose arrows.

Kiefan came up beside me. "Here!" he called again, and I heard someone approaching.

Ulf came on the scene from the other side, and stopped short for a moment. Then he grimaced and knelt to pick up the bow.

"Can you track them?" Kiefan asked.

Cords rose on Ulf's neck. He covered his hawk's eyes with one hand and fought with his answer for long heartbeats. "We can't leave the others long enough," he said eventually. "And all we'll find will be pieces."

My throat knotted too tight to speak.

Kiefan put a hand on Ulf's shoulder. Voice thick with emotion, "He died defending us. The Shepherd will give him a place of honor."

Ulf held his tongue and avoided looking at me when he stood.

The six of us regrouped at the kir fount while the lamia sang in the distance. It was a little pool between the thick roots of pines, fed by a spring at the deep end that burbled in a little fountain. The water glowed warmly, in the shade, and threw off bits of rainbow where it tumbled. The moment I laid eyes on it, I was thirsty. We humans dipped handfuls from wherever we could — Anders hopped across for more room — and even just a mouthful soothed and strengthened. The ponies shoved their way up to the little creek that ran down to the pond and drank from that.

After slaking our thirst, Ther Boristan said a few words for Bjorn, our brother disciple who we had known only a short time, but now owed much to. I kept my eyes on the toes of my boots, wiping away guilty tears.

Then there were wounds to see to while the men filled all the water skins from the spring. I cleaned Boristan's gash with plain water and, taking another gulp of kir, laid my hand on his wound. The lamia's fang had sliced across his collarbone, tearing wool and flesh alike and laying the bone bare. Bjorn's arrow had found the beast's heart a moment later.

I called the fresh kir up and it came, rising in a warm tingle in my chest and flowing along my arm to my hand. It drew up the disrupted patterns of kir in Boristan's wound until I could see them clearly. Lines and whorls of colorful kir moved through his flesh, through all flesh, in a set pattern. Wounds and illness disrupted the patterns, and

44

though the body would work to repair its patterns the process was slow.

From my Blessed memory, I took the correct pattern for skin and muscle in a simple area such as the collarbone. Flicks and twists with my mind shaped my kir to match the memory. My charm flooded down onto the wound, overwhelming it, and the flesh responded. The gash knit together into a red weal.

"Thank you, Dame Kate," Boristan said, checking it as best he could. "Heal the wool, too?"

I shook my head. "I haven't studied cloth."

"Perhaps I'll have a chance to do it myself."

Ilya's bite, on his calf, was more serious. When Acorn bolted along with Puck, Ilya had run after both ponies and been pulled down by a lamia. Ulf's arrow had taken it between the eyes. Anders had held three of the monsters off our pack-laden ponies when they'd been pinned between the pond and the stream's headwaters. One lamia was dead and the other two had run.

Rolling up Ilya's hose to his knee, I prodded the half-dozen half-crusted tooth marks. They still bled a little. He bit his lip and hissed through his teeth. I had seen a dog bite like this, a year ago, and Master Parselev had put my hand on his so I could see how he mended the patterns. I took another drink of kir and called it up. The muscles of a calf were far more complex; a meridian shot through the bundles of whorled kir, and the disruption the fangs had caused put up a fight.

As I worked, the frozen instant of Bjorn under the lamia's jaws, his muscle tearing, flashed past my eyes. A damaged knot of kir slipped out of my focus and danced away, jostling its neighbors and unsettling their dance. Ilya tensed with a curse as the jostle propagated in a ripple, knocking whorls together and tangling some. I countermanded it with more kir and the proper pattern, but it was spreading outside the part I'd seen under Master Parselev's guidance.

Grabbing a water skin, I took another swallow of kir and put my spare hand on Ilya's other, unhurt calf. Using that for reference, I halted the spreading damage. I combed through Ilya's tangled kir again, careful, and checked the patterns against his other calf. It took longer than it should have, and he'd found a stick to clench in his hands for when it hurt.

"I'm sorry," I told him, rolling down his hose over the lingering bruises, "I didn't mean to be so sloppy."

He managed a smile. "Still better than limping and slowing us all down, m'lady."

Puck, poor Puck, had a wound on his flank but Anders knew how to use a simple blood-stop charm and had already seen to it. I put my hand on the scabs and merely cleansed it to be sure it would heal quickly. For a moment, I glimpsed an entirely different dance of kir in the pony's heavy muscle. His skin shivered under my hand as it lingered there, remembering how Puck had spooked last night when the lamia charged. An echo of my own fear raised gooseflesh on my arm.

"Careful, he doesn't like that," Anders said, taking my hand from the pony's flank. "He's still a bit skittish after the bite."

I glanced up at him, mind far away, and I felt a blush rise on my cheeks. "I'm sorry, Puck," I whispered, and turned away.

"Are we ready?" Kiefan asked, striding down the half-assembled line with one hand on his sword. "Do we have all the ponies? And will we not let them bolt next time? There are pageboys in the castle with a better grip."

Ilya's face went white. "M'lord, I'm sorry," he blurted, dropping to one knee as Kiefan passed. "I let the fount distract me, m'lord. It won't happen again."

Kiefan stopped to hear the apology, then looked to me with a sharp glare like those he'd used on the first day.

It was a cold knife through my chest. I'd run. After all the orders to stay together, I'd bolted like a foolish pony. And Bjorn had suffered for it. He was dead now, when he'd been pointing out signs of elk and naming birdcalls this morning.

My eyes brimmed with tears that knocked loose at a blink. My failure, when I'd been charged with their care. I tried to whisper, "It won't happen again."

It didn't quite get out. Kiefan stepped closer, brows raised.

The lamia's green eyes as it pounced filled my mind. It wasn't half as bad as the blood spraying loose while Bjorn screamed. I focused on Kiefan's eyes and told him, "It will not happen again."

His head cocked, but then he acknowledged it with a nod, turned and gestured to Ulf and Boristan at the front. We walked on, past the

46

burbling kir fount and its happy twinkle, up the steep hillside beyond the pond.

———————✢———————

After the horrors of the surgery during the disaster at Ansehen, my master had taught me a trick of my Blessing. Something like a charm, a self-healing. While my feet moved and my hands held Puck's bridle — I'd taken him from Anders without a word — I dragged up each panic-fueled moment of the ambush and studied it. There were lessons in each one. Kir patterns, anatomy, physiology. Details about the lamia, such as the faint stripes on their forelegs. I looked at each bit of information and named it.

Once studied and put away, like blankets in trunks, those memories would behave themselves and come when called. Only when called. Though in dreams they slipped from their trunks, sometimes.

It was best done while lying in bed, but I had to keep up. Puck was very patient with me even though I kept leaning on him. I wasn't entirely aware of the others, but it seemed that they checked on me, concerned, and Ther Boristan said something about this happening to physicians. He walked with me, after that.

When I closed my eyes for a long moment, letting it all slide away, and then looked over at him, Boristan's brows rose. "Are you with us?"

I nodded. "Thank you. I needed to put it away."

Even though I had topped off with kir, I was tired. And that night there was little sleep to be had. The lamia stalked around our camp, keeping the horses jittery, for hours after dark fell. When the near half-moon Shepherd and his four Flock finally vanished behind clouds and it began snowing, the lamia left us in peace.

———————✢———————

The morning passed in silence; for hours, nobody wanted to speak. But then Anders grew impatient when we had to turn at a steep, rocky hillside and look for a gentler slope to climb up. Even in the afternoon sun, the snow underfoot wasn't melting and I know the chill was getting into my fur-lined boots by then, if not everybody else's.

"At this pace we'll miss the jousting tournament, if not the Solstice," he declared, throwing his hands up. "I'll lose my title by forfeit — and I'd rather be unhorsed by a green squire than that!"

Ilya called back over his shoulder, "You won me three crescents last year, Sir Anders."

Anders gestured back. "You'll win a dozen when I make it three years in a row."

"Nobody's ever done it, m'lord."

"Just you tell everyone you heard me swear I'd do it."

"Are you swearing, then?"

"By the Father's bloody —" Anders' volume dropped off suddenly when he remembered me, beside him. "— sword?"

I chuckled, knowing what he'd meant to say. "I've heard worse than that, sir."

"A maiden's heard worse than 'by the Father's bloody balls?'" He feigned outrage. "I'd never think physicians were so coarse."

"I might have even met some bloody balls while working the surgery."

He chuckled. "It's amazing where you find bloodstains after a fight like Ansehen."

"You're the tournament champion, then? Twice over?"

Anders dipped a quick bow. "At your service, m'lady."

"I hadn't realized it was you. I never saw your face, and everyone called you the Green Knight." Those cool, clear days at the beginning of the Hunter's Moon came back easily; the knight in the dark green tabard who unhorsed every opponent he faced, then fought them to a yield on foot. Repeat champions were rare, at the great joust — knights came from all over the kingdom to compete. They made their reputations, and their whole careers, in just a few days.

"The Green Knight?" Anders frowned. "Everyone in the pavilion knows my name."

Oh. "I've never been to that side of the field, m'lord." The tall, flag-bedecked pavilions at the joust were for the lords and ladies. I had been enjoying a rare day off with my family on the peasants' side of the field.

He smirked, caught in another mistake with me. "You've taken so easily to noble rank, m'lady, that I forgot. I hope you found the tournament thrilling?"

"We cheered ourselves hoarse," I said. "There are few days off, for apprentices, and it was thrilling indeed. Though I winced whenever a knight took that tumble off his horse and feared he'd break his neck. It must be harrowing to be a knight's wife at the joust. Save for yours."

It was a fair joke, and we both chuckled at it. Anders drifted a little closer, as we walked, and said, "No lady for a simple knight errant, though."

I found that hard to swallow; a handsome knight and twice champion, unwed? "A betrothed?"

He still shook his head. "What father would want a son with only a sword and a horse to his name? I'm sure you've done better yourself."

That touched a nerve. "No, I'm not wed. Or betrothed, not anymore."

"Anymore? What man would decline the apprentice of the Elect? Not only a fool, he's blind as well." Anders' eyes narrowed with a sly smile. "There must be a story there. A love story?"

I only shook my head and said nothing. When I last saw my father, we'd argued about my betrothal again. And then he had died at Ansehen, taken by fever when he should've been safe from swords and arrows. I would never make peace with him on how the betrothal had fallen apart. That fight haunted me still.

Anders' smile faded. "Did I offend? I didn't mean to."

"No, it's nothing you said." I clutched my cloak shut with one hand, to keep from fidgeting, and nearly tripped on a twisted little pine. The trees weren't much more than bushes now, the forest giving way to heath. My feet were cold and starting to dampen, too, from the snow soaking in.

Anders tried to touch my shoulder, getting closer still. "You're troubled. Don't say you aren't."

It was kind of him, but I shook him off and angled away. "My feet are cold."

He chuckled again. "If you need warming, just say the word."

That only soured me further. I quickened my stride and headed up the line past Acorn and Ilya and Boristan. At the front, Kiefan led. Ulf scouted the forest ahead, as he often did. I fell into Kiefan's pace at a polite distance, focusing on the rocks and fallen branches we had to navigate. No path to follow, up here. It had ended at the kir fount. This was barely a game trail through the brush.

The corner of my eye caught Kiefan looking at me, sidelong. After a time, he said, "Sir Anders has that effect on people."

"Does he think of anything but foolishness?"

Kiefan shrugged. "Not from what I hear. This is the most time I've spent with the man, in truth."

It was a day to learn oddities, it seemed. "You don't know the man, but trusted him enough for this mission?"

"The saints named him, as they did me. Putting all else aside, Sir Anders is one of our best knights. It rankles many, you can believe that."

That made me think of their sparring on Saint-day. The prince of Wodenberg had three Blessings, I had heard — speed, anticipation, and strength — and was the only disciple so blessed. Anders had only the first two. "He bested you in your skirmish."

"True. Rare that I meet a knight who can, though I think I saw a weakness in his guard... well, in any case, little time for sword training of late. Or reading." Pausing, he looked at me afresh and asked, "What of your reading? If there's some part of that Arceal you have questions about, I'm sure you can quote it to me."

I smiled and he echoed it. "True, I can. And there are a few parts I meant to ask about."

CHAPTER 6

I woke, even in the bedroll sausage-row, from the chill cutting through my blanket and cloak when the wind spun up to a howl. There was nothing to see but blue-white snow all around, and that was driving into my eyes. There had been no trees when we made camp, and the roofing tarp was far lower this time; when I sat up to rub my eyes, my head brushed the oilskin.

The wind shifted the snow away. I peered toward where the campfire had been and saw only shadows and blizzard. The ponies, tethered near the lean-to and wearing their blankets, were one mass huddled together against the storm. No sign of the fire, so what light there was had to be some sort of dawn.

As I watched, another form emerged from the driving snow. Kiefan crawled under the tarp on all fours, shedding flakes as he went. To me, "Good morning," and he shook Ilya by the shoulder. Sleepy noises came from under Ilya's fur-lined hood and blanket.

"Time for your watch, near as I can tell," Kiefan said. While Ilya muttered his way awake, Kiefan added, "If you're going out, don't go further than the other side." He indicated the tall bush that the upper edge of the tarp was tied to. The lower edge had been staked to the rocky ground. "Anyone gets lost in this and we'll need all Qadeem's wits to find them."

Ilya rolled over and lifted himself up on his hands. "Snowing?"

"And the fire died. You'll need a charm to get it going, if at all. Wake us at the usual time, or your best guess, and we'll see how the storm looks then."

"Can't walk in this, m'lord," Ilya commented as he crawled out of the sausage-row.

Kiefan spread out the bedroll that Ilya left behind, over the sleeping neighbors, and climbed into the spot before the wind stole all its warmth. When he pulled the ends around himself, I helped him get his feet covered. He shot me a tired smile before he pulled his hood deep over his head. "Maybe we'll get a little extra sleep out of this."

We did. The storm whistled and howled long after light came. We ate trail bread and used one of the heating charms we'd brought to melt a pot of snow to drink. We'd save the water from the fount until we needed it. We huddled around the heating charm until its kir ran out.

Then in half the time I'd ever seen a storm end, the blizzard was picked up and carried off by a stiff, icy blade of wind. The tarp rattled under the blast, smacking me through my bedroll and cloak. Sunlight glowed on the oilskin. The wind eased.

The sun was high and winking through fast-moving clouds as we struck camp — nearly noon, and Ulf urged us to be quick. The snow was ankle deep, powdery, and carried on the persistent breeze. I walked alongside Acorn, my hood up, mittens on, cloak pinned shut to my waist. Once out in the sun and walking, I warmed up and the day was clear and beautiful, in truth, though the breeze kicked up to a wind and threw snow in our faces every so often.

We stopped early to rest, and I was glad to. I brushed snow off a rock and sat to catch my breath. Without trees, the snow was a brilliant sheet laid over the slopes around us. I shaded my eyes and tried to look back, but we'd come around the shoulder of a hill and the valley was gone. Ahead a lumpy expanse of white rose until a sharp line of blue sky took over. In some places dark rock jutted, too vertical for snow to cling to. High up, the peaks loomed around us.

Kiefan checked on Puck and Anders, and in walking back paused to look up with me. "Ulf tells me that is Himmelbaum," he said, pointing back toward a snowy peak. Northeasterly, ahead of us still, "That's Starknadel. The pass goes over his flank."

"And where is this?" I pointed at my feet.

"The eastern side of Himmelbaum. Ready to walk?"

"It feel that we only just stopped."

"Ulf says we need to cross the valley while the wind is low. And this is as low as it gets."

My cloak swirled around my legs and the breeze pulled open the gaps between my cloak pins. We crunched across miles of snow, and if it was a valley I could hardly tell. The white hid all clues, and the sun washed out any lingering details when he emerged from the clouds. When I saw Ulf, his hawk's eyes were irised down to pinpricks of black. He scouted out a crevice in the rock, one with a ring of stones and a little ash still inside. It was deep enough for us and the horses, and sheltered enough that the snow hadn't filled it in.

"I wanted to be sure we found this camp," Ulf said. "In the spring, the snow melts a bit here and we hunt mountain sheep before they shed their winter coats. They supplied the pelts." He put a gloved hand to the lining of his hood.

"Glad that we did, it's a good site," Kiefan said, and coughed. "Glad we found it early, I was nearly forced to call another rest stop."

"Saps a man's strength, this cold," Ulf told him, patting him on the shoulder. "Call a rest whenever you need to, m'lord. And take a sip of kir, that's why we filled all the skins."

The morning sun had gotten a few rays in underneath the leading edge of the storm, then disappeared. We'd retreated to the safety of the crevice, out of the rising wind. The ponies seemed just as happy to have Ilya and Anders unload the baggage again. Blankets on, they idly licked the green lichen off the rocks while we kept the fire going with the last of Boristan's firewood.

We talked about hot summer days while the blizzard screamed.

Kiefan said that in the summer Dame Aleksandra, captain of the King's Guard, drilled him with sword and shield, in full mail and padded gambeson until sweat blinded him. "She called for cups of pickle brine," he said. "I thought she'd gone mad, but one taste and I downed the cup. Then I begged for more."

Ilya talked of the forge in the castle's barn-yard and pumping its bellows while the smith heated iron. Anders had a story about chasing a mischievous colt for miles in the middle of the Summer Moon.

When they came to me, I had no summer story worthy. The men expected I would tell them something about picking flowers in sunny fields on lazy summer days, and I got a good laugh from that. The laugh made me dizzy and then I started coughing. Ilya passed me the skin of fount water and I took a sip. The kir eased the cough and the creeping chill.

Ulf had brought a pack of cards and we played several games, brushing stray snowflakes away and coughing now and then. Boristan left to relieve himself and when he returned he was red in the face, breathing a bit hard for just a short walk and back.

"Do you feel ill?" I asked. "Feverish?"

He laughed. "I'm too cold to feel feverish."

Still, I put my hands on his face. "A little, perhaps."

"Your hands are cold."

True enough. I rubbed them together and put my mittens back on. The fire died in the afternoon but it was too soon for another of the heating charms. We kept playing cards until the shadows deepened. The blizzard raged on, and the snow outside grew deep. The wind skirled along the mouth of the crevice and carved the bank's inside slope into a smooth wave.

Once it was dark, Boristan triggered a heating charm to thaw out trail biscuits and heat some water to make bergamot tea. I was surprised they'd brought a little box of it in the baggage, but it was comforting to wrap my hands around a warm mug and sip.

Though we hadn't walked at all, I was still tired enough to sleep. The stone was just as cold as the previous night. We huddled close, and didn't bother making anyone stay up on watch.

When light returned, the snow had slowed. It was even falling almost straight down. Ulf went out to climb higher for a look, and came back a long while later with bleeding hands. "Slipped on the rock," he said while I dug out a cleansing charm from my medicine bag. "The clouds are breaking up, so let's head out."

The charm was bound to a wooden cameo of Mother Love. Ulf cupped his hands under it and I focused on the kir knotted up inside it. I imagined squeezing the knot and felt it give. The cameo glowed faintly and the kir dripped onto Ulf's wounds, banishing putrefaction from the flesh. My master had told me I would understand the why of that, someday; for now, I did it for knowing cleansed wounds healed faster.

"Thank you, m'lady. Just bandage them up and all's well. Save your kir."

———————————✦———————————

I crashed into Acorn's rump before I realized we had stopped, bounced off, and landed on my butt in the knee-deep snow. The jostle set off another round of coughing, and that knocked my sore head around too much. I'd meant to get up, but the throbbing convinced me to stay down.

At the pony's other end, Ilya plopped down in the snow too, chest heaving. Another stop to rest, thank the Mother. My feet were numb and the damp crept in despite my oiled leather boots. Head throbbing, I tipped back and lay on the powdery snow. My eyes fell shut. Perhaps I could get a little sleep before Kiefan started us marching again. Perhaps…

"Dame Kate? Are you hurt?" Kiefan landed on his knees beside me, pulling my hood open.

Startled, I batted his hand away and half sat up. "No, no, I'm sorry. Only tired and sore and…" I pulled off my mitten before it got to my forehead. The headache needled out from the foremost nubs of my Blessing, and kneading them helped.

"Headache? Me too. Take a drink, it helps." Kiefan offered the skin of kir-water.

I pulled the stopper and drank. "You said that Master Parselev wouldn't have told me about headaches? Your headaches?"

There was a tightness around his grey eyes and a crease in his brow, I could see now that he was close. "There are larger things to worry about," he said. "Frostbite. Storms."

The sky overhead was as blue as if clouds did not exist.

"You worry about the storms and I'll worry about the frostbite. And your headaches. They strike often?"

"Often enough. But since we left the city, not a one until we were snowed in."

"Does Master Parselev give you something or use kir?"

"I don't trouble the Elect with my headaches, most of the time. Don't trouble yourself with them either. One more sip and it's Anders' turn." He indicated the water skin.

55

"If you won't trust me with the truth, I'm no use as a physician." I took one more sip.

Kiefan considered that for a moment, and glanced toward Ilya who watched as he lounged in a snowbank. In Arceal, the prince murmured, "It's unwise for a leader to be weak. If there's a private moment, ask again."

That would have to do for a promise. I passed the skin back and he carried it down the line to Sir Anders, who seemed to have fallen straight into a nap the moment he sat down. Kiefan lightly cuffed him and held out the skin.

———————✕———————

A bit of wind was all the warning we got; icy needles crackled on my cloak and a curtain of snow swept through the pass. All but the rocky slope an arm's reach away disappeared. Acorn stopped. The wind rose further, whistling, then shrieking. I put my hands on Acorn's packs and pulled myself between the pony and the stone wall, slogging through the unbroken snow as best I could. I got as far as his shoulder and threw my arm over to hug him. I met Ilya's arm, there, as he'd done the same from the other side.

My head pounded as the wind wailed on and on. My throat was dry from panting, but I couldn't stop. I scooped up a mouthful of snow to eat.

The wind's voice trembled. Then it dropped, and the pelting ice slowed. Sun broke through and the squall pushed down the pass. The curtain of snow lifted as quickly as it had fallen.

I looked across Acorn's neck at Ilya. He laughed, shaking his head. "Do we get a moment's rest?"

"Can you see Kiefan?" Rock blocked my view, and I wasn't tall enough to lean over the pony.

"Boristan's lying down," he said, and took a seat in the snow. "M'lord should take another rest, he's been breaking trail all day."

Acorn shook his head, scattering ice crystals. I pulled myself to the pony's rear and stepped back into the narrow lane of trodden snow. Behind us, Anders was sitting too, Puck's reins in his hand. My mouth was cold from eating snow, but my throat was drying out again. I picked up another bite from a fresh snowbank.

"Dame Kate! Kate!"

At Kiefan's call I shuffled around Acorn, nearly stepped on Ilya's feet, and trotted up the line. Boristan tried waving me off with a mittened hand, but Kiefan tugged his arm down. "I'll be well. Just a few minutes to rest," Ther said as I crouched down beside both of them. "All I need is a few minutes."

Kiefan only tugged Boristan's hood back so the sunlight hit his face. He was pale, far too pale, and gasping for breath. I put my fingers to his throat and his heartbeat raced in his veins.

"He tried to stand and fell," Kiefan said.

"Just a moment's dizziness." Boristan tried to wave that off too. "I'm tired. We all are. Who can sleep well on cold stone?"

Ulf arrived from somewhere ahead. He'd been helping break the trail, to guess by his snow-plastered cloak. He breathed hard, but his color was much better than Boristan's. "We must press on," he said. "We're near the top of the pass, and well beyond where anyone's lived to tell of it."

Boristan clutched Kiefan's shoulder. "Help me, then," he rumbled, trying to heave himself up. Kiefan picked him up easily and held on when Boristan tried to stand alone.

"Can you break the trail a while more?" Kiefan looked to Ulf, who nodded. "Ilya! Up!"

I wasn't so sure it was merely fatigue. It looked like an illness, and we all had it. Cold, dry air and we were a small group in close quarters... I had seen how typhus fever rippled through the army as we marched to Ansehen. On cue, my chest tightened and I coughed as I started walking again. My pulse picked up and throbbed around my Blessing. A frown settled onto my face as my feet slogged on through the snow. I wished I'd found a walking stick while the forest was still with us. I wished —

"M'lord!" Ilya called. "M'lord, stop! Sir Anders!"

Kiefan turned and I did too. There was a thump as Boristan returned to the snowdrift and Kiefan trotted past, flicking a hand at me to follow. My leaden feet quickened and I followed his trail around Acorn, through fresh snow, back onto the path.

Puck stood unmoved, mouthing at his bit, connected to a dark mass in the snow by two reins. "Anders!" Kiefan yanked him up roughly and he startled to life. "He's bleeding!"

I arrived in time to see the bright smear of blood on Anders' lip as he wiped it away. His hood had fallen back and he was the same ashy pale as Boristan. Breath rapid and shallow. I checked his pulse and it was high.

"I dozed off, that's all," he protested. "Dozed off and another fucking nosebl —" A coughing attack cut him off.

"We spent all day lazing around camp yesterday," Kiefan said, "and you doze off out here?"

By the crease in his brow, Anders had a headache too. "The snow's more comfortable," he managed to retort.

"Kate, do whatever you must," Kiefan said, stepping back. "Whatever you can."

I hesitated. "Boristan's worse off," I murmured.

A glare. "Ther Boristan can't hold off three lamia at once. Can you heal this or not?"

I looked at Anders, sitting there pressing his knuckles to his bleeding nose and heaving deep breaths. Kneeling in the snowdrift beside him, I put my hands on his cheeks — scratchy with four days' flaxen stubble — and called up my kir. Tingling warmth rose to my chest, and even that far off I felt an echo in Anders' kir. Not surprising he'd be sensitive, given his double Blessing. His eyes fell shut and he leaned into my hands with a weary sigh.

Kir glowed in my hands and my patient's colorful whorls came to the surface. I focused on their dance, my own eyes closing as well to clearly see the full structure of his chest. Slow and weak, the whorls turned rather than spun. A persistent wobble in one of his meridians caught my mind's eye. I knew that one from studying the pneumonia patients in the Order's hospital — it joined the lungs to the heart and the prime meridian along his spine.

My hand slipped under Anders' cloak, under his layered woolens to press against his breastbone and he startled with a hiss. Then, a weak laugh. "You could warn a man, ice-hands!"

The contact made it easier to focus on his lungs, where the kir should be strong and vital. Stronger than what I saw. Peering close, I saw no competing kir pattern, as in an illness. Nothing attacking, only the sluggishness of heavy congestion. Strange. Nothing in my memory could advise me.

Still, I could help; my master had shown me how to clear the lungs. "Take a deep breath and hold it," I told him.

I wove my kir into a mesh and drew it through both of his lungs. The phlegm, as it was not a living thing or part of Anders' pattern, peeled away and I scooped it upward. The body's urge to be rid of it came on fast and strong, so one must be quick. Anders twisted over, heaving, and got most of it out in a mass. A second hard retch and he spat in the snow.

His kir strengthened and his meridian steadied. When I opened my eyes, his color was better. A bit of his smile was back, after he wiped his mouth. His arm looped around my hips and pulled me to his chest.

"If the rest of you needs warming, m'lady, I'd be glad to repay you for the kindness," Anders told me with a teasing smile.

"Here?" I cast a glance at the snowbanks, the pony, and more importantly the other five of our party watching. I was quick to extricate my warmed hand from under his cotes. No need to dwell on the muscles under there.

"If m'lady insists."

He did let me go when I pried at his hand, but I told him, "You've been kind enough to me thus far, Sir Anders, though you make it hard to remember that. Couldn't you simply be the good knight who untangled me from the stirrup that first day?"

His teasing smile dropped. There had been a nerve to hit in there, unexpectedly. More soberly than I had expected, Anders inclined his head. "My apologies, Dame Kate."

My new name had settled in, but it still didn't fit. "My name is Kate," I said, looking to Kiefan to include him in this. And I raised my voice so the rest of my audience would hear. "Majesty was kind to give me a title, but I'm only Kate. I'm not anyone's m'lady. Certainly not after you've all seen me tripping over these damn braies in the bushes."

Dizziness struck when I stood, and I nearly fell over. Kiefan caught me. "Bring that kir-water," he called to Ilya. "So was it a fever, D — Kate? Pneumonia?"

"No, I've seen pneumonia often enough. It's not." I stood on my own and he let me. "I don't know what it is. Ulf said it was the cold, but it's something about the cold here in the pass."

They strung tarps from the rock to make camp. Kiefan had to hammer pitons in, as he had the strength Blessing to make quick work of it. But so late in the day, he had little kir left. He clung to the bare rock when the wind whipped his cloak into a flag, pausing with the hammer in hand as he set his spine against the blast. The next blow he struck had half the strength, but he beat at the stone until the pitons were set. Then he stumbled to the little knot of Boristan and me, letting Ilya tie down the tarps around us.

We took Kiefan in, between us, swaddled him in our wool and fur. I hardly had a chance to think it was the prince who clutched me close for warmth. Boristan had us both in his bear hug until the shivering eased.

The ponies were glad enough to huddle with us in the windbreak even though it rattled and thumped under the air's fist. Whether it was a storm or merely snow blown up in the gale, it was impossible to tell. And perhaps it didn't matter.

Bundled together in blankets, in the dim light, I checked feet and hands for frostbite. The kir-water skin was getting light, but a few sips gave me enough to thaw out sluggish kir in a few sets of toes. I was leery of seeing a damaged pattern slip my control when there was little kir handy, but it seemed to help. The hairiest of the feet put in my hands was hardly even cold. I almost laughed. "Whose is this?"

"Me," Ulf said, his other end off in the shadowy mass of us.

"Did you glue wool to your feet, or is this the usual?"

They all chuckled. "Wife says I'm half wolf," he answered, doubly a joke as he was named for the beast. "Threatens to put me out in the kennel if I'm not polite enough for human company. That's how I know it's time for another hunt."

CHAPTER 7

"It's sleet," Ulf reported, and that was that.

Despite all the walking and fatigue, our appetite ran low. We dozed in our windbreak — the wind had lowered, thankfully, though the rain splattered loudly on the tarp — without breakfast and ate only a little at noon. Anders hauled himself up to unpack oats for the ponies and returned as exhausted as if he'd walked all day.

"We've another two days of oats, at full rations," he told Kiefan, and dropped back into his slot in the sausage row. "The sooner we get them to grass, the better."

Kiefan sat at the outside end of the row, pretending to be untouched by fatigue or headache. He nodded. "Soon as it lifts, we'll go. I don't want to lose this day any more than you."

But we did. I unpacked my Arceal book and sat beside Kiefan, closest to the light, reading and asking him to translate some of the more tangled passages. At one part, Anders spoke up, in the language, and explained an especially odd phrase.

"It's something they say when they think you're lying, but they don't want to insult you," he said. "They have quite a few of those."

"And how would you know of that, Anders?" Boristan asked, in Arceal, and managed a chuckle before breaking into a cough.

He smiled. "There may have been a few horses involved in a deal."

"How often have you been to Temitte?" Kiefan asked.

"Only a few times, and as part of the Kaufmanns' caravan. I wouldn't say I speak Arceal well, but if there's swearing to be done I can hold my own."

Still, I made good progress on my reading. The sleet finally stopped too late in the afternoon to strike camp, and we had to spend a second night in that crowded, cold lean-to, coughing and sore. Boristan wheezed in his sleep as if he had pneumonia, but it still was not. The blanket of clouds finally broke after dark and the Shepherd filled the valley with light. The Grain Moon was three-quarters full and five of the seven Flock were scattered across the sky.

I said, in Arceal, "Shepherd, gather your Flock."

"Shepherd, though I stray you call me home." Kiefan continued the nursery song, in translation, looking up at the sky with me. Beyond the moons, the stars lay thick on the sky's blanket.

"Shepherd, lead your lambs back to hearth," I finished. We sat quietly and I looked over my shoulder at the sausage-row of men. Still in Arceal, I asked, "Will you tell me about your head pain?"

"Headaches." He supplied the word. "I have headaches. There's nothing more to it than that."

"Often?" A shrug. "But you must have told the Elect about them." Parselev was the royal family's own physician.

Kiefan looked out at the narrow, snow-covered valley. We were up on a shoulder, following a trail of rock instead of walking on the snowfield below. The wind cut hard, down the center. He said, "If I can't shake it, it builds over days. When it's too much, the Elect sees to it."

"How do you shake it? Willow bark?"

"A few days' peace. Sometimes a quiet ride up to Prohzgrad will do it. At worst, a bottle of brandy."

I considered that. "A quiet ride up to the mountains?"

"I don't know when I'd gone so long without one, until the blizzards began."

"Blizzards," I echoed. That was a new word, in Arceal. Kiefan corrected my pronunciation. "Is the headache bad now?"

"I can hold out."

We watched the Shepherd and the Flock until I dozed off sitting up. Excusing myself, I crawled back to wrap myself in my bedroll and join my wheezing, snoring companions.

I had taken Acorn from Ilya so that he and Boristan could lean on each other as they walked behind the pony. Ther did most of the leaning, in truth. He was still deathly pale. I kept looking behind to be sure that Anders was still leading Puck, too.

When I turned forward after one such check, Ulf was breaking the path out front and Kiefan followed to widen it. The crust of sleet had frozen solid overnight, and fought even a man's weight before breaking.

Kiefan simply dropped, limp.

I blinked, and then fear stabbed me. I ran, pulling Acorn up to a trot. "Ulf, stop! Stop!"

My master's training guided my hands. I rolled Kiefan over, put my fingers to his throat to find his heartbeat, then brushed snow from his nose and mouth. His pulse was high, his breath fast and shallow like us all. He shook his head, muttering, and squinted in the light.

"I'm all right," he tried to claim. "Let me up."

"No. Don't argue with me." I took his head in both hands, thumbs on the initial nubs of his Blessing, and called my kir. His surged back, glad to answer.

Unwinding headaches was one of the first healing charms taught to apprentices. One didn't need to know the proper pattern for kir in the mind — there was none. All minds were different. A tangle of kir whorls and maybe a meridian caught in the mess was the usual culprit for a headache.

Kiefan's kir was knotted, hard and tight, around the meridians that sprang from his Blessing. He'd been shrugging this off for days? I'd never seen kir bound so firmly. I squeezed the knots, as one would an object-bound charm, but they didn't respond. Pressing a knuckle in with a twist, I felt one loosen. I reached for a second knot, did the same, and knew I didn't have enough kir to force all of them open. They were tough little nuts to crack.

He'd used half his day's kir, as it was nearly noon, and in my mind's eye the remainder hovered nearby in a glowing mist. Nearer than it should, in truth, as if it wanted to help. Mentally, I put out a hand and it flowed up eagerly. I picked the knots open one by one and the whorls tumbled out, confused and weak. The last of Kiefan's kir washing over them helped restart their spinning dance.

When I opened my eyes, fatigue fell on me like another cloak. They'd all clustered around to watch, sitting in the snow.

"Is he well?" Boristan asked. "You took longer, it seemed."

"I believe he is," I answered. Kiefan's eyes were open, under my hands, I realized. My thumbs were still on the roots of the two horn ridges that broke his scalp. I wiped away drops of melted snow, there.

"That's where they start," he murmured up at me.

"Did I get all the pain?" I asked. "You were full of knots."

Kiefan's smile was tired and thin. "That was amazing. How'd you use my kir? I'm not charm-handed."

Only charm-hands could donate their kir, unless one were Elect. "It wanted to help," I said. "Let Ulf and Ilya break the path today, for a change."

Anders took the chance to interrupt. "If you're not going to cuddle afterwards, we should keep going."

That got him two glares, which he laughed off. Ilya passed us the kir-water. The skin was light in my hands; I only took a sip and gave it back.

For once, we woke to the same weather we'd slept with. That alone brightened the day. Before we struck camp, I spent my kir on Anders' re-growing congestion and then took Ilya's through his charm-hand. That I spent on Boristan, and he perked up considerably after a lung-clearing — though he did complain that my hands were cold when I put one on his chest.

It was only more snow to look forward to, but we went in good spirits. The shoulder path lowered toward the snow that filled the valley. We met with rockslides from seasons past and picked our way through the rubble where we could. It took a little digging, at one point, and a heating charm to melt the ice that held the mass of gravel together.

But the happiest moment, by far, came in the afternoon as we forged through the calf-deep snow at what seemed to be the bottom of the valley. The shelf we'd followed through the pass had given out for good, but the snow had been knee deep up there. From up ahead, we all heard Ulf shout, "M'lord! Come see!"

He'd been scouting ahead now that the snow was shallowing. We followed his trail at a trot through a jumble of hillocks of rock and snow, finding him at last on the edge of a flat sheet as big around as my father's cottage. And we all heard it. Running water.

A frozen pool, that flat sheet, and a creek burbled out from underneath to run downhill. Its ice-crusted path led us, cautiously, down a ragged stone slope and around one last berm of avalanche rubble. There we stopped, stunned by the view.

The rock ran level for a hundred feet or so, more or less flat, and simply ended. We crept toward the edge, leaving the ponies behind, and sat within a few feet of the cliff. It fell away, as did the suicidal stream, far enough to make me dizzy when I peeked over. Ice glittered on the granite face below.

It was the view of Caercoed that held us there. Pine-forested piedmont gave way to a forest aflame in full autumn glory. Gold, orange, and red hills rolled north and east, interrupted by lakes here and there. On the shore of the near lake, a dark smudge of a village had pushed back the forest. From the center of the village rose a single, scarlet-cloaked tree in a gentle spiral, arms thrown wide as if in a dance.

"Tree's three hundred feet if it's an inch," Ilya said.

Ulf pointed into the distance. "There's another one, another village. I can make out three or four more, in the distance. The forest gives way to prairie, it looks like, but the trees still mark villages."

I could just make out a taller red head in the sea of gold and orange. The rest hazed into the distance, unless you had hawk's eyes.

"And there's the start of your grass, Anders." Ulf pointed closer. "Tomorrow afternoon, if we can find a way around this cliff."

When we turned, the ponies were already licking the lichen off the nearest rocks. We set camp behind the rocks and Kiefan assigned watches for the night again. I was glad just to wash my face in liquid water, even if it was ice cold.

───────────✕───────────

The third day after we found the cliff, I clung to Puck's back as Anders led him down a slender trail. My fever had been high enough, that morning, and I'd coughed out enough phlegm, that Kiefan had picked me up and put me on the pony. I hadn't fought it much. Puck's saddle wasn't meant for riding, but I wobbled along with two

65

handfuls of the blanket and saddlebags on either side to fall against. Anders kept a close eye; he'd wanted to tie me down.

Addled as I was, I felt Puck stop, take a few more steps to come alongside Acorn, and stop again. The men clustered in front of the ponies, muttering and looking ahead. I craned my neck enough to see a small pond and a clearing, through the thick screen of gold and orange leaves.

"Archers in the trees, I'm sure of it," Ulf said. "Well camouflaged. They've waited all day, I'd bet."

"They saw our campfires these past nights." Kiefan looked toward the clearing. "And since we stopped short of their ambush, they must know we suspect." A pause. "We didn't come to start a fight."

"Why are they in the trees, if not to kill us?" Ulf asked.

"Armed strangers wandering your forest? What would Baron Eismann do?" Anders asked.

"Saint Woden told me they knew we're coming," Kiefan said.

Boristan put a hand on our prince's shoulder. "Let me go in first, m'lord. Maybe they'll talk."

Kiefan grimaced, but nodded and stepped aside. Ther Boristan walked into the clearing, hood down, cloak behind his shoulders, and hands open. Stopping to cough up phlegm and spit a couple times, he followed the path to the well-worn patch at the pond's edge. He nearly got there before an arrow hissed into the ground beside his foot.

"Stay where you are!"

The accent was strange, but it was Arceal. Boristan stopped.

"Where 'tis you travel from?"

Ther answered in kind. "We came through the Eispitzen, by Starknadel's pass, from Wodenberg. Our saints charged us with finding the land of Caercoed. Have we found it?"

There was a pause. "Your leader must present and disarm."

Boristan looked back. Kiefan shifted his cloak over his shoulders and strode into the clearing, unbuckling his sword belt as he went. Sheathed blade in hand, he spread his arms wide. He'd started wearing the boiled leather breastplate again after the cliff, but aside from that he looked the part of a traveler.

"Name yourself."

"Kiefan Weissberg, Blessed knight of the Trinity, prince and heir to the kingdom of Wodenberg. I seek an alliance with the High Crowns of Caercoed against our mutual foe, the empire of Arcea."

A single word, and an arrow hissed. I saw only a flash of steel and a broken arrow tumbling to the grass. Kiefan spun his sword over his hand and pointed up into the trees. Where the shot had come from, I assumed. "Does Caercoed fire on the unarmed, then?" he asked.

"Legends must be put to test, must they not?"

Kiefan returned his sword to the sheath and spread his arms again. "So how should I test the legend of the amazons across the mountains?"

I didn't see the huntress until she stepped into the sun; her mottled cloak matched the shadows, her leather jerkin the tree trunks. A glimpse of short golden skirt had stood in for autumn leaves, over dark hose. She carried a bow, but un-nocked the arrow and returned it to her quiver.

The other half dozen archers who emerged did not, though.

"Peace-bond your weapons and we shall take you to —" and she used a long, bumpy word I didn't know. "Be welcome in Tadhlon of Caercoed."

'Tay-lon,' it sounded like to my ear. I leaned toward Anders to ask, "Who are we being taken to?"

"It's a noble rank, something like a margrave," he answered. "The Margraves Gwatcyn."

"Captain Mohra Fionmaen." She introduced herself to Kiefan with a bow. "Is your companion well enough to ride? We've horses." The captain indicated me with a nod.

"She can ride double. How far is it?"

"Come noon tomorrow, we reach Faen, where soft beds and mulled cider await the weary."

———————————✕———————————

I dissolved into the hot bath. Fire crackled on the washroom's hearth, heating another kettle of water if I wanted it, and noontime sun slanted through the gap in the curtained window. The clay tub was long and deep enough for me to lie in, if I folded up my knees, and I let myself slide to the bottom with my hair fanning out around me.

Near two weeks' sweat had crusted in places I didn't want to dwell on. We hadn't tried to wash on the Saint-day in the mountain pass, or even stopped for a disciple's dance. Now I picked at pimples and scrubbed with the coarse brush the maid had left me. The soap was lovely and smelled of rosewater.

When my maid, Anwyl, returned, I had gotten a layer of skin off and felt far more human. She wrapped me in a towel and squeezed out my hair into the tub, then pulled its plug and let it drain. Though she didn't speak any Arceal, she pointed me toward the fresh clothes I'd brought to the washroom and wanted me to dress.

After far too long dressing as a man, I was glad to slide into my light woolen shift and pull the drawstring neck close before tying it. While far warmer than the pass, it was still an autumn day here. My yellow dress, fitted more loosely and its neckline a broad, flat-hemmed scoop, went over my shift. Simply feeling skirts around my ankles again was a relief, despite that my dress was nothing like what the Caer ladies wore.

They wore straight-seamed, billowing tunics and tied them with a sash just under the breasts. The hem might be near their ankles, it might be at their knees, or just to their thighs, and worn over knit hose. Anwyl's tunic was knee long, and she wore hose as well. Her brown hair was twisted up in a simple bun and pinned.

Once my wet hair was wrapped in a small towel, she ushered me out of the washroom. Then I saw why; there was a line for the bath. As the washroom was just off the kitchen and its massive fireplace, so Kiefan and Anders and Ther Boristan waited on a bench next to one of the tables, watching the margrave's household chop and knead and roast. The girls who ought to be working were snapped at every few minutes for being distracted by the three strangers in the room, and every maid who hurried through stole an appraising glance.

The master of the kitchen, Aed, who was the margraves' husband, was not amused.

Anders said, "Hold on, I thought Kate was in the bath? Who's this, then?"

I know I blushed, and they chuckled, and Anwyl shooed me along back to my room upstairs. There, on the bed, she gestured for me to keep toweling my hair while she brought a small tea tray to my bedside table. When she lifted the lid to check the tea, it smelled wonderful and just like the blend Master Parselev preferred. All tea came from Arcea, so it might well be the same.

Anwyl picked up the comb and I untangled the towel from my hair, letting it fall down my back. When she only stood there, I glanced up, asking, "Is something wrong?"

Her eyes were fixed on my head, on my Blessing. She started to reach out with the comb, but hesitated and withdrew.

Nobody in Caercoed had a Blessing, from what I'd seen. As strange as it was for us to see women here, women there, only a scattering of men, we had to be far stranger to them.

I tried to look reassuring when I smiled. "Don't worry," I said, though she couldn't understand. "It only looks strange. You can touch it, don't be afraid." I took her empty hand and brought her fingers to one of the nubs, let her feel the cuticle where the ridge jutted up out of my scalp. "You have goats in Caercoed, don't you? Sheep? See how it feels like a lamb's horn nub?"

It took a moment, but Anwyl gently pressed. Maybe she'd been afraid the comb would tear the skin, as if it were a wound. Then she ran her fingers along the bumps, feeling how smooth and solid they were. Nothing to fear. I smiled with her as she said something, looking relieved, and then she sat down behind me to comb my hair.

I sipped a cup of tea, glad for its soothing warmth. A healer had visited me last night, after I'd been carried up to bed on arrival, and my fever and congestion had ebbed. The tea scalded some lingering phlegm from my throat. And though my hair was nearly long enough to sit on, Anwyl made short work of combing it out — far faster than my little sister, who couldn't stop chatting when she combed my hair. Anwyl began plaiting it without asking, some sort of braid far more complicated than I ever did, but I let her finish and tie the tail with a bit of cord.

There was a well not far inside the manor's gatehouse, with troughs for animals to drink and rough-hewn, sturdy benches. From my window, I watched water carriers line up buckets on the bench and one girl drew the water while the others took the filled ones, moved empties up the line, and hauled away when they had a matching pair.

Most importantly, the benches were in the sun whereas my room was a little dim for reading.

I tried to explain to Anwyl, but in the end she followed me and didn't entirely understand until I sat down and opened my book. Then she gestured to ask me to stay there. "Yes," I said, one of a few words of Caer I had picked out. I indicated my book and then the sun overhead.

That satisfied her and she went to see to other duties.

The manor's gate was ironbound wood, and the gatehouse a square tower on either side connected by a walk. Granite walls swept off in either direction, broadly encircling the tall manor and its outbuildings. The squad of guards at the gate noted all who passed through, but that was not too much excitement, it seemed. I caught them watching me a few times.

Kiefan sat down beside me, smelling of rose soap. Freshly clean-shaven, as well, he'd slicked his golden knight's crest flat between his Blessing ridges to his collar. He wore a black surcote embroidered with the royal sigil, a full Shepherd moon silhouetting Mount Woden, in snowy white.

He looked at me as long as I looked at him. "I must apologize. It had slipped my mind that you likely wear dresses most of the time."

"I'm glad to be out of cotes and hose. You men can keep them."

He smiled, watching the bustle of the gate-yard. "It's not so different from Baron Eismann's manor."

Chickens scattered as a wagon rumbled through, laden with fire-wood. Swirling dust picked out rays of afternoon sun. "Even with so few men?" I asked. "And those few in the kitchen?"

"It's strange," he allowed. "I'd heard the stories, but thinking of knights is one thing. I squired with Captain Aleks, after all, and she's been captain of the King's Guard for years. No man would dare question her strength or courage. One doesn't think that a land of amazons would be a land of carpenter women as well."

He gestured at the scene across the way, where a wagon minus one wheel was parked on blocks next to an open-sided hut. There, the carpenter carved new spokes for the broken wheel. She worked one stave with a draw-knife while shouting instructions to her apprentice, who cut more from a maple log.

"Why wouldn't there be carpenter women?" I asked. Bolder, "Why must men do everything? Women work as hard, speak as well, learn as quickly."

Some would laugh at that, but Kiefan only shrugged. Looking at my book, he said, "They do learn as quickly. I thought it ambitious of the Elect to give you such a book, but you soon proved otherwise."

I echoed the smile that crept out as he told me that. "I did?"

And for a moment, I almost thought he turned a bit shy when he looked away. "You're quite unexpected, Da — Kate." He corrected himself. "You asked to be Kate, so as you wish."

"I also wish you to tell me, next time, about your headache before your kir gets so tightly knotted." When he shrugged that off, I told him, "Master Parselev warned me about men like you."

Kiefan tried to appear wounded by that.

"Men who won't admit to pain," I said, "until they drop like a sack of potatoes on a snowy mountain pass. A few minutes could've put them right earlier, but no, they must press on."

He looked down at his hands, cracking his knuckles. "I'm the best heir Father has," he murmured. "I must be ready. My sister married Duke Seagrace and there are those who think my nephews unfit to stand in line to the crown. Will and Gerhardt are only boys, as well. And cousin Adalrich's crippled now..." His voice fell off further as he fidgeted.

"I regret that."

Kiefan frowned. "You? How — you were in the surgery." I nodded. "Adalrich said he owed an apology to the Elect for his language. You were out of pain charms?"

"So late in the day, none had the focus left for even a spark charm. Sir Adalrich needed three to hold him down, so it fell to me to amputate."

A nervous laugh. "You cut his foot off."

I nodded. "I'm sure it was only the pain that made him say such things."

"He hardly ever raises his voice."

"And had to be tied to his pallet to keep him from trying to walk, the next morning. That was when Master Parselev gave me the warning." I paused to check the memory. "He did say that all the king's kin were prone to it."

Kiefan turned serious again. "Leaders must pay their dues."

"You push yourself too hard." He started to brush that off too, and I said, "I know, it's better too hard than too little. But you're no use to anybody dead, either. I'm not going to tell anybody you get headaches. Saint Qadeem's rule honor-binds me."

Kiefan relented a little. "Next time, then. Shall we begin the second dialogue?" He pointed to my book, still open but barely read. We spent the rest of the sunlight sitting by the well, but only got through a few paragraphs. Our conversation wandered far and wide, and my thoughts slipped away every time his hand brushed mine.

CHAPTER 8

Mohra, the captain who had brought us to the margraves, collected us in a sitting room off the main hall as she'd told us she would. We six were clean and presentable, by then. She wore a uniform much like what the gate guards wore, a short version of the Caer tunic in beige, bound with a red leather belt at her waist rather than a sash under her breasts. The belt was for her sword. Her hair, it turned out, was short as a boy's.

"The Gwatcyns wish a dinner with you," she said, "ere the Crowns' Elect arrives. Likely, 'twill be on the morrow. They wish to welcome you as guests ere you are emissaries of your kingdom. There shall be no state questions, they wish me to tell you, merely curiosity. Bear in mind the family speaks Arceal passably well, even the boys — m'ladies do not believe in ignorance. Should you need a difficult translation, I will be at hand."

I wished I'd had a nicer dress to wear, not my old yellow thing with the ragged hem. A margrave was between a baron and duke in rank — far too polite a company for a peasant girl. I sidled closer to Ulf, who looked nearly as uncomfortable. Ilya and Ther Boristan knew more of such folk, and waited unruffled.

"No need to hide," Ilya whispered, nudging me closer to Kiefan and Anders. "His Majesty knighted you."

I nodded, as it was true, and took that step. But I clenched my hands together behind my back.

The ladies arrived and the Captain introduced them as Margraves Leix and Lorcana Gwatcyn of Tadhlon. At a glance, they were twins and dressed alike as well in full-length gowns of pale blue. M'lady Leix Gwatcyn served as a captain-general in the Crowns' army and had a

73

square-shouldered air about her. M'lady Lorcana smiled more. Both ladies wore their grey-streaked hair and faint crow's-feet with dignity and grace, and kindly acknowledged my attempt at a curtsy and the menfolk's bows.

It was when the daughters arrived, Aifric and Esgwen, that gave me pause. They came running down the hall outside chattering until a man's voice sharply stopped them. Half composed, they stepped into the drawing room door, pink-cheeked and fighting down giggles. They were twins as well, dark hair cut short like Mohra's, short-skirted and looking to be twelve or thirteen.

"'Tis well we could have one meal together ere the elect rides in," m'lady Leix said, in Arceal, as a maid handed out teacups. "Please, Captain, introduce our guests."

She began with our prince, then his guardsman and then, to my surprise, his physician. Lorcana said with a smile, "Healing is a lofty art in Caercoed. Is it so in Wodenberg?"

I curtsied again. "The highest calling of Saint Qadeem's disciples, m'lady."

"Surely it made your mother proud."

I could say, honestly, "My mother was proud, yes."

M'lady Lorcana's blue eyes narrowed, catching me. "But who was not proud?"

Everyone who understood Arceal watched me now, with curiosity. Especially Kiefan. I felt a blush creeping into my cheeks, but there was no helping the truth. "My father did not want me —" I began, but didn't know the word in Arceal. "Taught? By my master, in an agreement?"

Mohra supplied the word. "Apprenticed."

"'Twas your father who opposed?" M'lady Lorcana weighed that. "But did not prevent, else you would not be here."

"The piglet died," I said.

"A piglet?" Leix chuckled when she said it. "How did a piglet sway your father?"

"Father brought me home from the Order after my first two years of study, even though the Elect wanted me for his apprentice. An apprentice is for five years, so when I finish I will be nineteen. To be unwed at nineteen, even as a physician…" From the faint lines in their

74

brows, the margraves didn't quite see why that troubled my father. I risked a glance at Kiefan, but he studied his tea. Anders and Boristan were translating for Ulf and Ilya. "I am only an Englic peasant girl, m'ladies. Father arranged my betrothal to a blacksmith and clinched it with a sow piglet for my dowry. But she took ill and died when the snows came early. For want of a piglet, my Father signed the apprentice papers and I went back to the Elect."

M'lady Lorcana smiled. "How far along?"

"Two years, m'lady."

"You must be a bright star, to be trusted with such so young."

My blush deepened. Thankfully, attention passed from me to continue the introductions. Ther Boristan of the Order, woodsman Ulf and manservant Ilya were presented in turn. "Be welcome at our table, no matter how humble your roots," Lorcana told them and Kiefan translated. "You've crossed dire mountains and there will be no offense taken tonight. 'Tis a saga to tell, surely, Prince Kiefan?"

"It was a difficult journey, and we were glad to see trees again after so many days of snow and ice. And to hear wolves howl rather than lamia singing."

Aifric and Esgwen perked up at that. "'Tis lamia across the mountains?" one asked.

"Do you have them here too?"

"In the northern lands. A wonder your little ponies outran such beasts." The girl jabbed that at Anders, who only smiled.

"Our ponies are as valiant as ten horses," he replied. "They didn't even trouble themselves to run."

In the drawing room door, the margraves' husband Aed — whose husband? both? — cleared his throat and offered a slight bow. "Dinner is prepared," he announced. "'Tis an honor for my son Tiarnan and I to serve."

I wondered, for a moment, if the son had a twin too but no, only one boy about my age was in evidence in the dining room. Pale, delicate, and his hair was so dark it was nearly black. Tiarnan saw the guests to the table, and his father escorted the margraves and the daughters. The former were seated at the head of the broad table, the latter at the foot, and we guests in between. We each had a fine-glazed porcelain plate waiting for us, a matching cup, and a wooden spoon besides. The table was well lit by candelabras and evening light through the windows.

In our Alemannic, Kiefan asked, "What was that about the ponies?"

Anders sat across the table. "I checked on them, to be sure of their treatment. And I may have been looking at the other horses when the twins discovered me." He grinned. "I nearly had a chance to see their swordsmanship. They're fierce defenders of their favorite horses."

Kiefan stood and caught both girls' eyes with a shallow bow. "If my guardsman troubled you or your horses, m'ladies, I apologize."

I believe it was Aifric who fought down a laugh and Esgwen who stood and answered. "'Twas only a startle, sir. Though your guardsman was nosy as a horse-trader."

"Perhaps because I am a horse-trader, now and then. Most often a trainer of warhorses," Anders said.

That got them off and talking about horses, particularly with m'lady Leix who rode warhorses herself in the Crowns' army. As they talked, I ate by turns a bowl of potato soup and a plate-full of roasted chicken with greens. The dagger I had carried and eaten with through the trip suddenly seemed far too large and awkward. I tried to copy Kiefan's table manners by watching him sidelong.

The conversation subsided a few minutes when the apple-and-raisin tarts arrived and cups of brandy were poured. "Needs must ask," m'lady Leix said while Tiarnan cut and served slices of tart, "of the obvious, dear guests. Stories told by far-ranging caravans of horned men tend to put one in a mind of a man's natural horn." She chuckled at that along with my companions; I turned some shade of pink. "But I see 'tis not a mere turn of phrase. What 'tis that does such violence to your profile, Prince Kiefan? To look at it, I'd think 'twas painful."

"Blessings are bestowed without pain, m'lady. Once Blessed and claimed by a saint, we know our purpose in the kingdom. Some for war, some for wisdom, some for building," Kiefan said, reciting what we were all told as children.

"An alliance of three saints — a rare thing. Qadeem was one, you said?"

"Qadeem for wisdom, Aleksandr for craft, and Woden for war."

M'lady Leix paused in taking a bite of apple tart. "Saint Woden? Of Wodenberg."

"And the city of the same name, on the slopes of Mount Woden."

"Puts his mark on everything, does he? Aught else?"

"He is my grandfather, some times over," Kiefan said.

That was well known, that the royal family was descended from Saint Woden, but when Kiefan said it I happened to be watching Anders splash a little of the brandy onto his apple tart. And I remembered what Baron Eismann had said about sending both... claimants to the crown? Now that Anders was cleaned up and out of that deep-hooded cloak, I suddenly saw a bit of the resemblance. He was a little older, lighter in the hair and bluer-eyed, but he and Kiefan shared a jawline and cheekbones.

Everyone said that the queen hated the king because of the bastard son that'd come after her two princes died. Before Kiefan.

Anders leaned back in his chair with his doctored slice of tart. He wore his uniform, a black tabard embroidered with the cavalry sigil, for knighthood, two golden stars for the Prince's Guard, and a brass ring knotted on each epaulette to indicate a sergeant's rank. Jousting champions were always promoted to the Guard, and he'd won it twice.

Kiefan had said the saints assigned Anders to the mission, and he hardly knew him. Why?

I had lost track of the conversation with the margraves, but m'lady Leix managed to catch my ear. "You mean to say that all your people are Blessed? There are no laypeople, no disciples?"

Ther Boristan answered. "We are all disciples, m'lady. We are all part of the kingdom, we are all bound to the cause of the Trinity."

Lorcana said, "But not all have the gift of kir. In Caercoed, as in many places, only those who prove sensitive are discipled by saints. Of those, the stronger rise to the rank of blessed and perhaps on to elect."

"Some Blessings are greater than others," Boristan offered. "I have only a minor Blessing, myself, but I receive my due share of kir and use it to serve the saints."

That seemed to be a new point. "Your due share?"

"Yes, daily, for my Blessing. And if I don't require it, I can use it in a charm."

77

The margraves' eyes tracked across each of us, newly wary. "'Tis quite an arrangement your Trinity has, dear guests," m'lady Lorcana said, in low tones. "If you are all so blessed, there must be so many elect that you could hardly need the aid of Caercoed."

That deepened the silence. The answer itched in my mouth, but I didn't think it my place to speak. It was Kiefan who said, quietly, "Wodenberg has only one elect for the moment. Elect Parselev, Dame Kate's master."

Another long moment passed, and Leix broke the silence. "I do apologize, dear guests, for I promised no questions of weight tonight. 'Twould seem that we should arrange for sparring, for I've heard from my guards that they're eager to see how such knights handle a sword. And if the woodsman is willing, 'twill be archery as well."

"Tomorrow is Saint-day," Boristan said, "and there'll be training for certain. We missed a Saint-day, up in the pass, so we'll all be following instruction this week." With a stern look, he repeated that for Ulf and Ilya. "Washing, disciple's dance, and all." They muttered a bit for having to wash again so soon, but it was half-hearted.

"Fortunate, then, Elect Tannait will be here tomorrow," Lady Leix said. "She'll wish to see these war Blessings at use."

I, for one, was glad for the chance to stretch in the disciple's dance.

We drew an audience in the gate-yard. M'lady Leix and her daughters watched, as did several squads of guards from the barracks and as many housemaids as could sneak away from their duties. Caercoed had no Blessings, no Saint-day and no disciple's dance — when Captain Mohra told me as much, I had to wonder just what the Caer saints gave their people.

After the dance ended, wooden swords and round shields were brought. I sat on a bench outside the kitchen with the captain to watch the audience as they watched the knights. Aifric and Esgwen wore their own wooden training swords and stared, rapt. Two littler sisters had come out to watch, too, a pair of six-year-old girls. Twins.

I had to ask. "Mohra, I noticed that... oh, your pardon," I began to apologize; I had been in the wrong language.

She only smiled. "'Tis long enough now that I've picked up your tongue," she said in Alemannic. "We have Blessed of our own, in Caercoed."

"How many do you speak?"

"Arceal, Suevi, Ryu and now — what do you call this?"

"Alemannic."

"Ah. Not so different from Suevi. I speak Englic, too," Mohra said, switching again. "Could have a truly private conversation. You're Englic, yes? By your name, I thought you were."

"Yes, but I only speak Englic at home," I said, lowering my voice. Ther Boristan and Ilya weren't far away. "It's not used in Wodenberg."

Mohra nodded. "Few Englic ships make the north crossing, the old timers say, since Wodenberg took you." But she returned to Alemannic. "What 'tis you meant to ask?"

I indicated the margrave and her daughters. "The ladies are twins. As are Aifric and Esgwen. The two little ones as well? Are twins so common, here?"

A laugh escaped her. "All girls are twins in Caercoed. Saint Conbarre and Saint Sabh bestowed it on us."

"Twins as well."

"Naturally."

"Is your twin a captain also? Blessed with languages?"

She shook her head. "She's a disciple and sees to her market stall. Our husband keeps house and raises our girls."

I wanted to ask about that too, but Kiefan and Anders finished their training forms and began their sparring. M'lady Leix and some of the officers shouted out requests in specific swordsman's terms. The two men stripped off their surcotes, as the afternoon was growing warm, and faced off in their closer-fit, plain wool cotes. At first, neither used his speed Blessing and they merely showed off their swings and jabs and blocks. But then they shifted into a true blur and held it longer than I'd seen before. Wood cracked on wood, on flesh, and when they slipped out of speed both their chests heaved. They circled, guards high, and Anders lunged in to set them off again.

Leix leaned to the nearest of her officers to ask something; the woman only shook her head. The skirmish lapsed out of Blessing speed when Kiefan stumbled back from a hard jab to the shoulder, gritting his teeth. I didn't see the counter-strike, nobody did, but Anders' sword skittered away on the packed dirt and he shook his arm with a grimace.

"No need to truly disarm me," he said, loud enough to carry.

"M'lady, Captain?"

Tiarnan Gwatcyn stood in the kitchen door. He took a few steps toward us, fidgeting with his hands until he clasped them behind his back. The knee-length surcote he wore looked old-fashioned, to me, and the apron over it was streaked with flour. "Think you that they'll want some tea? Or perhaps ale? Once they end their... swordplay?" he asked.

"Mayhaps you should take a sword and try it yourself, m'lord. You're sure to know what they'll want then." Captain Mohra smiled, teasing.

Even the lightest touch of pink showed, on Tiarnan's pale face. But he was handsome enough, in his quiet way. "'Twould be foolishness, Captain. M'lady, would you care for tea?" That with a smile that had to fight its way out.

"Tea would be very kind of you," I said, managing a smile back. First knights and princes, now a margrave's son offering me tea. Stranger and stranger.

"Oh, 'tis no trouble. Not for a master of the healing arts."

"I'm hardly a master."

Tiarnan was quick to shake his head. "On such a journey through the Iawyr? When you faced lamia? I've mended but a few fevers, splinted a broken bone — I cannot imagine, m'lady. I would tremble in my boots."

"I did some of that myself."

"Surely you..." Tiarnan trailed off when he looked in the direction the captain jerked her chin. He closed his mouth, pressed it in a thin line.

Kiefan had the practice sword across his shoulders and gripped in both hands, using it to casually massage a muscle or two as he crossed the yard toward us. He didn't say a word, he merely took an extra step closer to Tiarnan to make it clear the margrave's son had to look up to meet the prince's gaze. Not a glare, not a twitch in Kiefan's face, but Tiarnan looked away quickly and retreated into the kitchen.

80

I didn't notice that until he was half gone, and felt a twinge of sympathy. "He was asking if we'd like some tea."

Kiefan stretched both arms up and back, sword for a spacer between his hands, and his joints crackled a bit when he let go, swung the wooden blade down. "Tea? Water would be enough."

Mohra chuckled and leaned close to my ear to whisper, in Englic, "Lucky girl, to draw that one's jealousy."

My mind stumbled over that. Kiefan said, "Pardon, Captain?"

"How does one train at such speeds?" she asked him, instead of answering. "And how long does a day's kir last, spending it on speed?"

"One trains at ordinary speeds and the mastery carries over. The second's for me to know and my enemies to fear."

I felt a tickle, a faint shiver in my kir, and I would have thought little of it if Kiefan and Captain Mohra had not both looked toward the gate with me. "Do you feel that?" I asked.

"Must be the Elect," Kiefan said.

"Yes, 'tis." The captain stood and called to m'lady Leix, then at an order trotted toward the gatehouse.

Anders wandered over to my bench as well. "What chance of getting a drink of water while they prepare, do you think?"

I chuckled as I got up. "If he hadn't been frightened off, we might've had some." I went to the kitchen door and leaned in.

Tiarnan looked up as he turned out a lump of dough from its rising bowl. The mass deflated as it landed. "M'lady?"

"Might we have some water, rather than tea?" The words were strange in my mouth, asking a gentle-born man for something so plain. But he obliged, and still had time to knead down his dough, return it to its rising, and join us in the gate-yard before the Elect arrived.

Four riders trotted in, but my eyes went to Elect Tannait the moment she was in view. She was a small woman, when she alit from the saddle, but she let her kir draw eyes and hold them. It was nothing so obvious, not the kir fount's glittering or glow, merely a warmth under my breastbone and an inability to overlook her. Master Parselev usually wrapped his kir away, and said it was a good trick to know when you wanted to go unnoticed.

She went first to Leix and Lorcana, accepted their bows and kiss of fealty on her hand. The Elect wore her hair loose and it shone steel-grey in the sun, but her face was ageless like my master's. She walked directly to the six of us next, not waiting for the margraves' introductions, and looked up at Kiefan with narrowed green eyes. She didn't say a word as she went to each of us.

I meant to look her in the eye, when my turn came, but kir moved, plucked mine in my chest and it answered like a bell. My breath caught. It bloomed white in my mind's eye, singing out a few clear, strong notes. The blossom subsided but the chord hung in the air. Elect Tannait could hear it, I didn't doubt, but nobody else seemed to. A tiny nod was all she gave me, and moved on.

I'd felt that once before. Elect Parselev had done it, bit his lower lip a moment, and said I would be his apprentice.

Ilya, last to be inspected and the most nervous of us, was the one she said something to. Captain Mohra stepped up quickly and translated, "She asks why you came here."

That bewildered the poor man. "I came to serve m'lord. M'lady."

Another question, which Mohra translated as, "'Twas your free will?"

"Of course, m'lady."

She asked the same of Ulf, who answered, "I was asked to lead m'lord through the mountains, and was honored to."

Boristan said, in turn, "The abbot told me Saint Qadeem wished me to keep a book of the mission, and I was honored to."

The Elect went to Anders next, and asked her question. "This sounded better than haying —"

A slender vine of green kir shot from the Elect's hand and cut him off with a firm grip on his jaw. Her eyes narrowed. I saw him swallow and look away from the elect's eyes.

"My saint ordered it."

She said, "You might have refused."

Anders stared into the distance and held his silence. She waited. Her grip on his jaw tightened. A wince twitched at the corner of his eye, but still he said nothing.

Tannait coiled her kir away and moved on to Kiefan. "It was my duty," he said.

She measured him for an extra moment, but did not ask about free will. Then it was my turn. "My master sent me," I answered, before she asked.

Her kir-vine grabbed my jaw, strong as any man's hand. I tensed — it was an honest answer, I knew. Tannait asked, in Arceal, "Why was it you?"

The answer bubbled up, called by her tight grip. For a moment, I hesitated, but saw no reason not to answer. "Master said it must be me."

Tannait nodded. "'Tis an interesting bouquet your saints send." She beckoned the margraves closer, to include them in what she said next. "'Tis the saints' business that brings us here. They have their own concerns and have made their own arrangements. 'Tis for us to manage the remainder. Questions on both sides, no doubt, that it falls to us to ask and answer. The first of these: how many elect does Wodenberg bring?"

Kiefan answered. "One."

That surprised her. "One? Not ten? How many Blessed?"

"All of us."

Tannait nodded. "I see. 'Tis a wager of a different sort. You bear the most of these — Blessings — what are they?"

"Anticipation, to know my enemy's attack before he swings. Speed, to strike before he does. And strength."

Her head cocked. "How strong?"

Kiefan took his practice sword in both hands — fine, strong oak, thick as my wrist — and snapped it like a twig. Then he took the two pieces in his hands and broke them together. They resisted only a heart-beat. The margraves' eyes went wide for a moment, then recovered.

Tannait only smiled. "Please, dear guests, continue your sparring for us. Leix, find us your best swords to join in. Do you have a Blessed in your guard? I trust these knights are too polite to embarrass them."

———————✟———————

There were many questions over the next two days, as the Grain Moon waned. I was privy to some of the meetings, and some of them Kiefan told us about while we sat around the kitchen fire after dinner. The kitchen fell quiet after all was cleaned up, and the Gwatcyns with-drew with Elect Tannait to their private den and their own fireplace to share their own thoughts.

Little had been said, at home, about the state of Wodenberg's army after Ansehen. I knew we left a broad field covered in dead men, but it wasn't for a physician's apprentice to know what that meant. Killing Arcea's elect had cost the kingdom thousands of lives, none of them easily replaced. Arcea, though, was a vast empire with lakes of kir and a host of elect to channel it through. Their elect's last attack had destroyed much of the fortifications on Wodenberg's southern border and our first line of defense was little more than an inconvenience now, as the raiders at Gabel had proven.

We had a kingdom of Blessed, fearsome on the field, but only one elect — and him a healer.

Caercoed had held off Arcea's armies at the two southern mountain passes that bordered Suevia, and knew the empire's power well. They had fought the same kir-forged monsters that Arcea's saints produced. Caercoed understood, and they were even impressed that we had faced an even number of Arceal and won, however narrowly. Caercoed used its strategic advantage of the passes, its defensive engineers' wits, and its strong elect to win against Arcea's monsters.

"Our Trinity has kept to themselves, Elect Tannait said," Kiefan told us, swirling the brandy in his glass. "And being good neighbors, Caercoed's saints did not press the matter as there was little contact across the Eispitzen. Arcea conquered Suevia fifty years ago and then had to see to its own southern border. Now they are turning their eyes north again and seeing the kir founts in Wodenberg. Wanting them.

"Our weakness is how close the fount on Mount Woden is to our border. The battle at Ansehen weakened our southern army. Father sent orders to Duke Seagrace late in the Summer Moon: collect the northern reserves and come south. Progress reports have been good and they'll march from Rukharbor in the spring, soon as they can, but armies are slow. Even cavalry. Arcea will swarm the fallen wall and arrow for Wodenberg. Any aid Caercoed can give to slow them, or hamper the siege they will lay on the city…"

There were stories of Arcea's sieges on cities in Suevia. Terrible stories. We sat in silence after that.

Anders had gained a pair of demanding students of horsemanship, in the margraves' daughters, and excused himself to bed each night after a quick drink. Kiefan would excuse himself soon after, and if a headache was twisting its way into his skull he took my hand and kissed it. I would put my palm on his cheek for a moment, enough time to pinch out the tangles of kir before they tightened into knots.

Kiefan would smile, and that always made me smile. I went to bed warmed by a few sips of brandy and the feel of his lips on my hand.

CHAPTER 9

"Yes, needs must. 'Twill be a traditional Caer interrogation, as Dame Kate is a woman. No harm will come to her," m'lady Leix told Kiefan. "Most likely, we'll be home ere midnight. Needn't wait up."

He shot a troubled glance at me, mittened and cloaked and waiting at the great hall's door between Captain Mohra and Elect Tannait. "There's little Kate could tell you that I cannot, m'lady. Whatever this interrogation is —"

"—'tis not for boys," she told him, with a pointed look. "If you worry on trust, consider that I trust you in easy reach of my husband and children." Turning, she gestured me out the door.

I looked back to Kiefan to be sure, and he nodded. Horses waited outside, held by Anders rather than one of the stable-girls. He gave me a boost up that I didn't entirely need, and while pretending to check my stirrup he jammed a sheathed knife between my boot and calf. As if I could fend off all my escorts with it.

Still, he was sincere when he whispered, "Be careful."

We rode out of the gate and down into the town of Faen, on the shores of the lake they called Ty. The last gloaming shone on clouds' bellies and the first stars twinkled in the blackening blue. Even in the gathering dark, the Mother Tree glowed red, rising over Faen with her arms thrown wide. The ladies led me under her broad canopy, and a red leaf fell near my hand. I caught it, tucked it away with a glance at the heavy branch above.

The tavern's sign was a maple leaf and a golden crown. A girl took our horses and I followed Leix and Lorcana into the main room. The voices within paused a moment when the door let in a gust of chilly air, but then they recognized the margraves and welcomed us with a cheer and raised steins. A waitress put down her tray of drinks to take our cloaks, smiling and bobbing a curtsy.

Elect Tannait put her arm across my shoulders and announced something that got another cheer. Half a dozen guardswomen who'd been lounging with their boots on the largest table quickly cleared out. I looked to Captain Mohra for a translation as I was steered toward a chair.

"She only told them 'tis to be an interrogation. Don't get many, here. Don't worry, Dame Kate."

I landed in a chair at the table. The tavern was warm, well lit and full of smiles; it smelled of mutton soup and autumn ale. The waitresses wore knee-length gowns, woolen hose, and kept their necklines sensibly high. Despite what m'lady Leix had said earlier, a man brought out a pair of small glasses and a large bottle of clear liquid. He put one glass before the margrave as she sat opposite, one before me, and the bottle in the center of the round table. He spared me a kind smile through a close-cropped brown beard. The tavern's patrons settled down again, dragging tables and chairs to a polite distance to watch.

I thought it was m'lady Leix opposite me, and glanced to her twin to check. But they were dressed identically, down to their hair tied back in buns, and I couldn't be sure at first. Elect Tannait picked up the bottle from the center and pulled the stopper.

Captain Mohra pulled up a chair beside me to translate. "These are the rules: both sides drink, the subject answers a question. If 'tis a worthy answer, the subject may ask a question."

The elect filled both glasses and stopped the bottle. "What sort of questions?" I asked the captain.

She nodded to my shot. "Drink and see."

It was cool in my hand and smelled like the triply-distilled spirits Master Parselev bought from a Russe merchantman and tucked away on a shelf in his office. The margrave — I matched the streak of grey by her ear to Leix's face, thanks to my Blessing — drank hers in one swallow.

Pressure touched my temples again and I glanced at the elect. She raised an eyebrow. Her kir-vine turned my head toward the glass. Our audience chanted one word, low and growing, that didn't need translating. The shot bumped against my lips and I drank. The stuff seared my throat.

M'lady Leix asked, in Arceal, "Surely you're not the sole apprentice in Wodenberg. Or your master the sole physician. How 'tis that he sent you, rather than one of them?"

One glass of the spirit felt like a whole stein of ale at once. It didn't give me the answer, though. "He said only that it must be me, m'lady. Nothing else. Even my saint, when they saw us off, said nothing of why. Only that he believed I wouldn't fail." The memory of Saint Qadeem's dark eyes was a sudden weight on my shoulders. He expected me to succeed. I hadn't even known what to succeed at.

"And you did not fail."

"I failed when the lamia ambushed us. I ran, and Bjorn died for defending me."

"Still, you've given a good answer. Ask your question," Leix said.

"About what?" I looked to Captain Mohra, who'd been handed a stein of ale by a waitress.

"Anything," she answered.

I thought I'd hold them to that. "Why did you want to question me alone?"

"Needs must have the truth of your menfolk's ways," m'lady Leix answered, as if it were a simple thing.

Elect Tannait filled our glasses again. M'lady drank hers without hesitating. I looked at the glass, wondering what they'd ask next. The pressure returned to my temples, prodding me, and I drank.

"If 'tis right, I ken you're sixteen now, Dame Kate, and were fourteen when your father wished you wed. How 'tis your father didn't wish you the honor of apprenticing to your kingdom's only elect?"

Father had told me why, at the top of his lungs, when the piglet died. "He wanted me safe." It made my throat thicken, to remember that fight. He'd thought I'd murdered the piglet, at first. "He was right, I suppose. Nothing safe in crossing the Eispitzen."

That got a murmur of agreement from the audience when Captain Mohra translated. Leix said, "Ask your question."

A glow was creeping into my chest, and it wasn't kir. "Would it be different, were I Caer?"

"Most certainly. 'Twould be an honor for any daughter to be

apprenticed of an elect. At any age. If Aed said aught 'gainst it, I'd consider, but…" m'lady Leix shook her head.

"A father's will means nothing?"

It was a second question, but she answered while the Elect poured. "Fathers are for kisses and sweets. The mother who bore you knows the truth of life." Leix picked up her shot for a toast in Caer, then repeated it for me in Arceal. "To hearth and home and the boys who keep them warm."

That sounded nice enough, I had to admit, and toasted along with the guards.

Her next question was, "This husband you'd have had — 'twould have allowed you to study?"

I had seen it happen often enough with other apprentices to answer. "Perhaps. I might have gotten another year before falling pregnant." My fluxes hadn't come until I was nearly fifteen. "After that, what time is there? Half Mother's luck, in being a midwife, was having an eldest daughter at home while she was seeing to deliveries."

M'lady beckoned for more. "I'm only a peasant girl. Gentle-born wives may study more, if there's a wetnurse for their babies. Servants to cook dinner." Thinking of the morning in the Chapel, I mused, "The king may have knighted me, but I've little to my name but my Blessing."

She was nodding now. "You play this game well, Kate. Ask your question."

"Husbands, in Caercoed," I began, and had to think a moment. The question slipped away in the warm haze, then circled back. "Whose husband is m'lord Aed?"

A grin. There was a bit of pink on m'lady's cheeks, perhaps from the drink, perhaps not. "Why, 'tis our husband. We courted him, each in our way, we came to love him, we married him. 'Tisn't always thus. Had we not agreed, one of us might've taken him as consort instead."

"Consort? Leaving one sister unwed? How…?"

"Our brother Oisin is a consort. Crown Ceelin's very fond of him, and he's given her fine princesses. Crown Ciara's kind, but isn't so inclined. She has her own lovers."

Elect Tannait unstoppered the bottle for a fourth time, held it up and began to sing. The audience immediately joined in, leaping up from their chairs to dance in time with the rollicking tune. Captain Mohra swept me up by the elbow and I was spinning, tripping, trying to regain my feet. She didn't let me fall. I went on a complete circuit of the table and I had almost caught up as the song drew to a finish. The last note was held a long time, with laughter, and then I had only a moment's glimpsed warning before she leaned over and kissed me.

Not a chaste kiss.

And she deposited me in the chair again, my knees gone wobbly. The Caers all picked up their steins and cheered, then drank. My glass was full again and m'lady... I tipped my head, frowning. She was picking up her glass, raising it to me, and then drinking.

Kir-vines nudged me, pulling my eyes to the Elect. Drink. The glowing green kir sprouting from her hand unsettled my stomach a moment but I was playing the game well, Leix said. I couldn't be harming the mission. I emptied the glass.

"You're peasant-born, Dame Kate — we have none, in Caercoed, but 'tis common in Suevia. Arcea keeps slaves. What means it in Wodenberg?"

"I must obey my lord," I said. She beckoned for more. "Whatever my lord commands, unless it goes against a greater lord, I must obey. My father obeyed Duke Seagrace and came to Wodenberg as part of his retinue. He helped build m'lord's manor in the city, helped furnish it. Father was a master carpenter, and m'lord was pleased with his work." That gave me some pride. Father had always been proud of it.

Then I realized Captain Mohra was translating, as I'd lapsed into Alemannic. "Your pardon, m'lady," I said, my face catching fire. "I forgot myself."

"'Tis no concern," Leix said. "Should m'lord order you to his bed, must you obey?"

That made me blink. I'd never so much as met Duke Seagrace. "M'lord?"

"Your Prince Kiefan, say."

Though my face still burned, a shiver ran down my spine at the thought. The kiss Mohra had given me, from Kiefan...? My pulse rose.

Beside me, she chuckled and leaned toward one of the guardswomen to whisper something. The other grinned, a wicked glint in her eye, and agreed.

90

I found the answer, while part of my mind was still caught on kisses. "The Mother's discipline binds us, m'lady. No lord should ask, and any maiden should refuse. But m'lord might bargain with her father. Contribute to her dowry, to maintain her marriage-worth after. Any good man would do so."

A hush had fallen on the room when I finished. "Would you be weddable?" Leix asked.

"Most any girl is. It's only a question of who. But Father is dead, and I'm a Physician now." I sat straighter in my chair. "I have my virtue and I'm still weddable even without that damn piglet."

"You certainly are."

Elect Tannait poured me another drink as I leaned back in the chair. I watched the clear spirit splash out, thinking of the kir fount and its glow, how its sparkle cut the light into rainbows. Captain Mohra handed her empty stein to a waitress and declined a fresh one. My lips still felt that kiss, as did my tongue.

"Why did you kiss me?" I asked.

She smiled. "'Tis what you do at the end of the song. Want another?"

My face had only just cooled and it heated back up. "I only ask because it was so... different."

"Never been kissed, even?" Apparently, that was amazing. "I'm glad I fixed that, then."

"I kissed Harold, once," I said in my own defense. "He stole one. I let him."

"If you get through this and the next, we'll sing again." She smirked and indicated my full glass. I turned back to it and I was listing. Or else the table was. Gripping the rim in both hands, I straightened us both.

"You're doing very well, Kate," M'lady... she didn't have the grey streak by her ear. M'lady Lorcana said. She held up her glass. "You're being a great help."

She drank, so I had to. I could barely taste it anymore.

"Five days you've been our guest now. Do you think a wedding 'twixt Caercoed and Wodenberg could be happy? Could your Prince Kiefan wed one of ours?"

I leaned back in my chair again. Five days. I had watched m'lord Aed and Tiarnan run their house and kitchen, precise in their expectations but kind when need be. Never had I eaten so well or so much. My shift was getting snug. A chuckle burbled up out of my warm glow, jiggled me in my seat. "Don't expect him to cook, m'ladies," I managed to say.

They chuckled, and there were some comments in Caer and laughs.

"What?" I asked, looking toward one of the speakers. "What?"

Captain Mohra told me, "Only that they'd be willing to cook, if one of those knights waited in bed."

"Dame Kate." Lorcana pushed through the mirth. "Do you think the Caer too different, too… wild, to be wives? In Wodenberg."

"Wild?" I echoed.

"Some have said that."

I looked to the uniformed guards again, their boots on the tables, not minding that their braies showed where their hose ended. That they wore braies at all would be odd, in Wodenberg. "Saint Woden does claim some women for knights, m'lady. The captain of the King's Guard is Dame Aleksandra — I haven't heard her family name. Ask Kiefan, he told us that she squired him. And that no man can question her courage."

We didn't drink again, but we sang the song in any case. I tried to get out of my chair for the dance, but fell against the table and Mohra caught me. She put me back in the chair and kissed me again at the end. Then she helped me out to a horse and into the saddle, and rode close beside me while the margraves spoke with Elect Tannait.

I hadn't realized that saddles were so slippery. The captain had to keep a grip on my arm.

The guards at the gate welcomed us back. My eyes hung half-shut, by then, and it was a good thing my horse stopped along with the others. I leaned on Mohra; she was solid and warm.

"Catch her?" she asked, and I blinked as she slid away. I flailed but fell only a little, into a pair of strong arms. The stirrups caught on my feet and I kicked at them.

"Hold still," Anders told me, shifting me higher on his shoulder, and the stirrups were pulled off my boots. "You have the horses, Tana? Doesn't look like this one should try walking."

"I can walk," I protested, swinging my feet down to try it. A few steps went well enough, but then one foot tripped on the other and Anders caught me.

As he half-carried me, by the arm and waist, toward my room Anders told me, "My little sister came home this drunk, once. I helped her sneak in, but then she threw up. Feeling anything like that?"

"I feel great," I said, lolling against his shoulder. "I'm supposed to sneak? I don't think we're sneaking."

"Well, nobody here can thrash us for getting drunk. No need to sneak."

My room was at the top of the stairs, at the beginning of the hall. The sight of my bed made me tired. "I've never been so drunk. Didn't even mind when Mohra kissed me."

"I'm sorry I missed that." The lamp in the hall cast a slice of warm light through my room, enough to stand in while Anders pulled back the covers.

I caught myself leaning too far and stumbled against the wall. Bed seemed like an eminently sensible idea, suddenly. "You're right, I should go to bed. But I should tell Kiefan what happened."

"You can tell him in the morning." Anders held out a hand. "Get some sleep first."

His hand was strong and warm when I took it, used it to steady myself as I crossed the floor. Then I remembered, "I should take my dress off," and started to pull my hems up.

"Don't worry about that now," he told me. "You're tired. Get in bed."

It was a nice, warm bed. M'lord Aed had laid on plenty of quilts and wooly blankets. The straw stuffing was fresh, I could tell by the scent when I fell onto it. I started to climb in and realized my boots were on. And what was stuck in my boot. "Your knife," I said, and lifted my leg up to get it.

Anders intercepted my hand, took the little knife, tugged my foot down and pulled my skirts back over my bare knees. "Got it. And your boots."

He untied them and loosened the laces. Nobody ever took my boots off for me, before. "You see? Like I said, you can be kind. Without all that foolishness."

Anders' voice dropped. "You're not making it easy."

From the door, Kiefan said, "I'll make it easy for you." He leaned against the sill, partly blocking the lamplight, arms crossed over the silhouetted moon on his chest. "You keep your hands where I can see them."

My boots slid off, one at a time. "And what's it to you, where my hands are?" Anders asked. "You can't be jealous of how quickly I got into her skirts. Unless..." He trailed off as he stood. I pulled my feet up before they got cold, and grabbed at the covers. "Unless you want her."

"Leave her alone. And go."

Anders stepped past him through the doorway, trading glare for glare. Kiefan put his hand on the latch and drew the door shut as he went, lip pulled under his teeth as he looked back at me.

———————×———————

"The Crowns' courier did bring word from Castle Adhalon," Leix told us. "She winters there, at Arforddinas."

She put her finger on the map spread on the table, on the coastal city nearest the southern tip of Caercoed. Below Arforddinas, the mountains and then Suevia. Kiefan had laid out our map of Wodenberg so that the Eispitzen overlapped Caercoed's Iawyr — as the two lines of mountains were one and the same. The margraves' town of Faen lay nearly due east of Vorspitz.

"They reaffirm 'tis my judgment where Tadhlon's forces march in the spring. I did neglect to tell you our brother Oisin is Crown Consort. When they were but princesses, the Crowns were as our younger sisters."

Leix had brought us all to this office, even Ilya and Ulf, who'd been working as handymen to keep busy. Ther Boristan sat scribing in his book, as he had at all the meetings, and m'lady Lorcana did the same. I stood by the table with hands clasped, not sure what my part was, studying the Caercoed map and trying to work out the place

94

names through the fancy script. The pounding in my head had eased a bit after a trencher of eggs and three cups of tea, but it was still hard to focus.

"The Crowns don't wish to meet?" Kiefan asked.

She shook her head. "Winter Court is hip-deep in plots and intrigue. To toss you in would be less than kind. Fortunate for Wodenberg, then, that Dame Kate answered so well last night and I'm partial to killing monsters. Are we to cross through your pass, Prince Kiefan? 'Twill be dangerous, come spring. Avalanches."

"There's a smuggler's trail," Kiefan said, pointing out the very southeastern corner of Wodenberg. "Our border here is steep hills, and guarded. If you push through your southern pass early and hook north, it will get you to Wodenberg. Though the danger may be equal. I'll write you a letter of introduction and give you some names — which must be guarded closely." He paused until Leix nodded in agreement. "My mother the Queen is Suevi, the last of their royal blood after Arcea's slaughter. There are those who will help, in Suevia, but they do it at peril of their lives."

"Why a letter of introduction? Come yourself. Be welcome to winter here."

"We leave soon as we can," Kiefan said, which caught everyone's ear.

A shiver shot down my spine, the echo of far too many days in that snow.

"The Grain Moon's waning fast, m'lord," Boristan said.

"All the more reason. The Leaf Moon won't be any warmer on Starknadel. The word must get to Baron Eismann and Margrave Schutze to redistribute their reserves. And to watch the smuggler's trail for your soldiers. They can see you safely over, if need be." Kiefan paused a moment. "And I must take the word to my father."

Leix pointed out, "'Twould be a pleasant surprise, riding to your city's relief with Caer knights."

I was only across the table, and I barely heard Kiefan murmur, "Father hates surprises." Louder, "I'm honored by your offer of hospitality, m'lady, but I must go."

Her grimace seemed honest enough. Leix exchanged a worried look with her sister. "'Tis only the marriage to discuss, then. The

Crowns have their consort and their heirs. The princesses are too young for such things, but there's others. Duchesses of age."

"I'm sure a suitable marriage will be the simplest of the matters," Kiefan said.

"We'll speak more on it in the spring. At your feast table." Leix smiled.

CHAPTER 10

Leave-taking needed another day of preparation. I'd recharged my blood-stops and cleansers; Ulf and Ilya had done the same with the warming charms. Puck and Acorn had enjoyed their week's sleep and good grazing, Anders reported.

Not even the autumn Equinox could keep Kiefan from beginning the trip home. The Gwatcyn's gate-yard was decked with banners for tomorrow's festival and the kitchen ran full tilt baking and roasting. We were squeezed down to a cluster around the end of one table to drink our brandy, that final evening.

Still, we had that chance to clear out our few grievances, as one ought to at Equinox. When light and dark balanced, one should balance one's accounts with the community. But most of our personal accounts waited at home; the mountain pass had bound us in close camaraderie, and we easily said all we needed to say. Quiet followed.

I only sipped my brandy, still wary after the interrogation's headache. Kiefan sat at the table end closest to the fire, writing on a sheet of fine linen paper. We watched him finish with his signature. "This is for my father," he said, folding it. "Should anything happen, it's this bag that must be put in my father's hands." It was a plain enough leather shoulder bag. Kiefan added the letter to its contents. "It's all here: Ther Boristan's book, letters from the Crowns and the margraves, a draft of the treaty. The list of marriage prospects. All of it."

"It's true, then? You'll have to marry one of these — ladies?" Ulf asked.

Kiefan buckled the bag's flap tightly. "It's hardly a matter of wanting." Bringing it with him, he joined us at the hearth and reclaimed the glass of brandy he'd left on the mantle. He took a deep breath of its fumes, then sipped.

"They're good enough shots with a bow, m'lord, and their cross-bows are impressive. M'ladies have been fine hostesses and I'd be glad enough to visit. But these brassy girls for wives?"

I had seen Ther Boristan's diagrams of the crossbows in his book. Ulf said they were powerful, and that was enough explanation for me.

"It's hardly a sacrifice, in comparison to what I asked of those who followed my charge at Ansehen," Kiefan replied. Sadness lingered around his mouth. "I only ask my marriage be peaceful. Mother Love knows that's eluded the king and queen."

Ilya spoke up in the quiet that followed. "They weren't always so angry. It was your brothers dying that drove them apart."

Ulf said, "We all grieved for the little princes, m'lord."

My eyes wandered to Anders, but he only studied his brandy. Even if it were true that he was the king's bastard son, it was hardly his fault. He'd had no say in the matter.

"We've an early morning," Kiefan said to break the silence. "Thank the Mother for your warm bed, tonight." As the other four made agreeing noises, he turned to me. "Kate?"

I let him take my hand and kiss it. When I put my hand to his cheek and called up my kir, I didn't see any tangles in him. "You've a headache? I don't see any…"

He put his hand over mine, pressed it with his eyes shut. "I wanted your touch."

The melancholy in his voice pinched my heart. "You only have to ask," I murmured.

Kiefan's fingers combed into my loose hair and drew me into a kiss, gentle and chaste but slow to part. I confess I tensed in surprise, held my breath. But my heart pounded.

"I didn't want to risk Starknadel without having done that," he whispered, near my lips. When my eyes opened, there was a faint smile on him.

The margrave's question flashed through my memory. Should m'lord order you to his bed — as if he would need to order, after the hours we'd spent studying d'Ovio Alain's dialogues together. My hand, which had fallen to his shoulder, trembled and I took it back. I knew what happened to girls with neither dowry nor virtue, despite my spirit-bolstered claim during the interrogation.

"M'lord, you know Father Duty's teachings," Ther Boristan said, perhaps a bit louder than need be. "A moment's fun is a poor trade for a lifetime's happiness. Not only yours — hers."

I looked, and they were all watching. Boristan frowned, Ulf seemed amused, Ilya's mouth was pursed and uncertain. Anders merely drained his glass of brandy and said, "I'm off to enjoy that warm bed."

"It's only a good-night kiss, Ther," Kiefan said, letting me go. To me, warmly, "Good night."

And he melted me all over again. I wanted another kiss, I wanted his arms around me. They thought the Caer were brassy? I was only a peasant girl, but dared to moon over a prince.

I murmured, "Good night. M'lord."

Next evening, though, I put the lesson Captain Mohra had given me to good use. And I did surprise him, though only for a moment and then his tongue was quite able to match mine. My skin throbbed where his hands had landed on my waist; I felt the pressure even through my layered boy's cotes. He'd seen me to the little lean-to I shared with the captain and another Caer, and they were waiting back at the campfire. I'd taken my leave a little early in hopes of precisely this moment of privacy.

"Good night," Kiefan murmured, lingering at close range for a tantalizing moment.

I hadn't realized my hands were trembling until his found them, squeezed them. That gave him pause, and I took the chance to try to swallow the tightness in my throat.

"I don't mean to frighten you," he whispered, shifting away.

The truth spilled out of me. "I'm frightened of myself."

Kiefan squeezed my hands again as he took a full step back. His mouth pulled to the side and he wanted to say something more, I was sure, but he slipped away instead. He left me alone with wild day-dreams to dispel as best I could.

Captain Mohra saw us up the hill as far as the frozen spring, two easy days on horseback with her squad cooking and setting up shelter for us. Frost sparkled every morning on the leaf-littered ground. The trees' flame-painted cloaks thinned.

Two days without another good-night kiss. My blood cooled a little, aided by a conveniently timed lecture Ther Boristan gave on Father Duty's lessons of discipline. I read a little more of my master's book and Kiefan helped translate, both of us on best behavior.

A mushy crust of snow had reached the bottom of the cliff face, and thickened as we rode up to the spring. At the top, the spring took some finding, lost as it was under snow and too frozen to flow anymore. I recognized the rocks near it. Captain Mohra doubted me, at first, for the scattered rubble all looked much the same.

"You remember the rocks?" Kiefan asked, a bit puzzled as well.

"When Ulf called us down, we stopped at the edge here," I said. Checking my memory, I pointed to two boulders that seemed to have noses and eyebrows. "Those didn't have any snow on them. There was a blue jay on the taller one." The bright flash of feathers had caught my eye.

He tipped his head now, curious. "What else do you remember?"

I checked my memory again. "Your cloak was sodden about a handspan from the hem. When you took a handful of water and drank, you noticed how thick the stubble on your chin was. Then Puck nosed you aside to get some water himself."

"I hadn't known you saw so much detail."

"I remember everything I see," I said. It was simple as that.

"And smell? Feel?"

"Yes."

Kiefan paused a moment. Voices called us to dinner at the campfire, and we started across the gravelly snow. "So when you cut off Adalrich's foot, you remember…"

"Everything, yes."

"What he said?"

"Why wouldn't I?"

"It sounded like what people say when they've forgotten," Kiefan said. "You remember taking — an axe?"

"Saw. Master Parselev had cut much of the flesh off, but then Sir Adalrich punched our orderly, put him down hard. Master had to help keep him on the table. I was the last free pair of hands. Fortunate that I'm a carpenter's daughter." I thought it amusing enough for a smile, but the prince looked a little pale.

"I still have nightmares of the charge, and it's only a handful of clear moments when I try to think of it. I doubt I could stand to have anything more," he said.

"My memories can be put away," I told him. "Like folded blankets. But I do have nightmares, now and then."

In the morning, we left the Caers to strike their camp and continued up the snowy slope. Ulf led, somehow finding the trail through ankle-deep snow — I knew it was the same we'd come down by, largely — and I fell into a dogged rhythm with my feet.

The first snowstorm hit us that afternoon.

We lost three days to storms, and hours to passing squalls. I only noticed the wind when it eddied for a moment, dropped enough that when it rose again it was a fresh knife across my face. My nose bled as I gasped for air, and froze more than clotted. We all coughed and panted and slogged as best we could through thigh-deep snow.

Kiefan helped me wash the blood from my face, using his bare hands to melt the snow. Then a kiss, just a quick, chaste one. I stared at him a moment, but he only nodded and said, "Good night."

Once we were up on the shoulder ledge again, against the stone face, Kiefan broke the path for us. I followed, leading Puck, and Anders behind me with Acorn. Ulf and Ilya took turns half-carrying Ther Boristan at the rear.

The nights were dark and frigid, and all seven Flock moons could not provide much light while the Shepherd waned to a sliver. Every night, we bundled up together with a heating charm in the blankets at our feet. I did what I could to clear the congestion, ease the headaches, spending all my kir and whatever Ilya could give me through his charm-hand Blessing. I got a little good-night kiss each evening, but exhaustion kept them brief. We didn't have flasks of kir to ease the journey, this time, though the Caer did give us what extra charms they could.

"To think the saints chose us for this," Ther Boristan said. The wind screamed, thumping the tarps against our bodies, and horizontal snow poured by our windbreak. "I thought them kind. Saints Aleksandr and Qadeem, that is. Saint Woden always seemed a stern master, to me."

Anders snorted, which started his cough.

"He is," Kiefan said for him. "Are they kind, then? The others?"

"You've a strength Blessing, m'lord, that's a claim by Saint Aleksandr," Boristan said.

"Not in my case. And here, not strong enough even with the Blessing."

"Nobody could ask you to be stronger," Boristan said, but at that Kiefan laughed until he coughed.

When he got his voice back, he said, "You haven't met my father? Was a time I thought he and Saint Woden agreed beforehand which Blessings I'd get. They have me so well corralled."

Ther seemed puzzled to have to explain. "No, the saints make their own choices. They know which Blessings fit you best."

Another harsh laugh. "I studied, when I learned about the Blessings, I read every book I could lay hands on. I learned Russe and Arceal and asked Mother to teach me Suevi. Believing that if I was ready, if I was smart enough…" Kiefan trailed off, clamping his mouth shut. "Child's dreams," he said. "Nothing more. Born yoked to the plow, so best to put my shoulder to it."

He said no more and after a time the conversation turned to home. The storm blew itself through the pass late in the day and we dug ourselves out as best we could with our two shovels. Blinding sun beat on the fresh snow for a short time before the shadows gathered. We ate a cool dinner of Caer trail bread, full of walnuts and bits of dried apple.

When I got my kiss good-night, I whispered, "You wanted Saint Qadeem to choose you."

He hesitated; it was something of a blasphemy. But Boristan's even wheezing marked that he'd dozed off, and Ilya's snore was unmistakable. The rest likely couldn't hear. "Yes. I wanted it even more, after. I hardly saw a book for all the sword training and jousting. Even asked —" Kiefan's voice dropped further, though I was huddled close. "I asked him why."

"You questioned Saint Woden?" I nearly tripped over the words in surprise.

"No — Mother have mercy!" He chuckled, and coughed a little. "I asked Saint Qadeem."

"What did he say?"

"That four Blessings would have been too much." Kiefan was lost in the memory, for a moment. "Said he would've been proud to have me. It was kind of him, I suppose."

"Saint Qadeem doesn't say things idly, Master Parselev told me."

Kiefan's mouth twitched to one side. "Still, if I'd been Blessed with memory, or with master-craft, or even just craft-handed, as Ther Boristan is, I would be better for it, I think."

It seemed a strange thing to say. "You hate the sword?"

"No. There's a grace, when my kir melds the speed and anticipation to the strength and the flow of it — but since I woke from my Blessing and found the sword was my destiny, there's not been one day I'd want to treasure."

That saddened me. Since my Blessing, studying at the Order had changed my entire world. They sent me home a few times a year and I was ashamed at how my feet dragged on leaving and flew in returning. My parents' little hut, which had been so cozy and safe, now reminded me of the hungry winters and threadbare clothes when there'd been little work for my father. "I wished for the heat-sight Blessing," I admitted, "when I was little. I thought I'd be a better cook with it. But now I wouldn't want anything but memory."

"If you'd gotten any other Blessing, I'd never have met you," he said. "Perhaps I'll have to admit to my headaches, if it's you who heals them."

My heart quivered in my chest, at that. "I might not see you again, otherwise."

"You'll see me again," Kiefan murmured, sounding half-asleep.

I wasn't so sure, and the more I thought on it as he drifted off, the more I doubted it. The ache of that kept me awake.

CHAPTER 11

The second day after, we stopped early to set up camp and all grinned as we did it. Ilya trotted off as fast as his coughing let him while Ulf unloaded the tarps and Anders found a place to tether the ponies.

Under the snow, the lumps around us were juniper and stunted spruces. The branches Ilya found were wet, but Boristan had enough kir for a fire-spark. "At least I can be some use," he said with a smile, stoking the flames carefully with grass and leaves. The branches caught slowly, smoking. Boristan coughed and had to turn away. "May not be cooking with this soon," he managed to add.

"Smoke is what we need," Kiefan said, watching the column rise off the little fire. The sky was clear, for now. "Smoke for a hawk-eye in Vorspitz to spot."

It was enough to melt some snow, bring it to boil and make some tea. Boristan was too weak to do more than manage the fire; I took the big skillet and cut up some potatoes to fry with a bit of ham. Below us, the forest rose up and blocked much of the view, but in the purple distance I could see Wodenberg's western mountains. The afternoon sun settled itself behind them as I cooked. I thought I saw a silver curve of the Neva River, out there.

Home. My eyes misted and I had to put the pan down to wipe them.

Dinner was simple but heavenly. The men praised my cooking until I laughed myself into a coughing fit. Since we ate early, I had enough light to clean the pan by, and stood wiping it dry at the fire while Ilya told us about his young daughter's coming birthday.

I saw Ulf cock his head, and both the ponies look up from grazing on tough mountain grass. "Bring them in! Close to the fire!" He scrambled toward the leads, tied to a stubby spruce tree.

Boristan, energized by the meal, hauled himself up to help. "I'll get Acorn."

Anders got up too. "Don't strain —"

Ragged snarls tore into camp and the ponies squealed. Dark forms streaked by and two hit Boristan full on. A glimpse of sword and shouting and the pain of the skillet hitting my foot knocked me back to sense. Screaming, and not just mine. Boristan's feet, kicking, dragged through the snow away from me and I leaped on them. I caught one ankle in both hands and threw my weight against it.

Two lamia had him, one per arm, shaking him, blood spraying, as he shrieked. One beast planted its paws and pulled. The other lunged at me and I let go on reflex, threw myself back from its yellowed fangs with a scream.

The lamia burst in half, innards spilling free; the second stumbled from the sudden freedom and then ran with its prize as if Boristan weighed nothing. I fell backward, through the campfire. Kiefan slipped from Blessing speed for half a second to keep from tripping on the monster he'd killed and was struck from behind, thrown down. That one didn't stop, it ran over him and caught Boristan's thrashing ankle, helped its pack-mate drag.

Ilya caught me, pulled me clear of the flames before my woolens caught. He hollered and I heard teeth snap. Then Kiefan was there, between us and two more lamia, bloody sword ready. Boristan's wails, fading with distance, spiked to a ragged scream that faltered and choked into horrible silence.

"Behind us, m'lord!"

Kiefan spared a glance over his shoulder and I looked too. Three more circled, across the fire. Their spiny hackles flexing, ratty tails lashing, they paced to and fro, eyes fixed on me and Ilya.

I gasped, "Where're the ponies? Anders and Ulf?" No sign of them but churned snow and the ends of broken leads on the spruce.

One lamia lunged, teeth snapping, but danced back quickly when Kiefan swung around the fire. Ilya had his dagger out and shifted up to his feet. His hands shook, but he pointed the blade toward the monsters. My chest heaving, head spinning, I fumbled for my own knife and clenched my hand on it. Useless, to me, but it was something.

It dragged into an impasse. The lamia circled us, teeth bared. One tried a dash at Ilya but Kiefan swooped around in a blur and the beast's ear went flying as it tried to dodge. With a squeal it fell back. Then another feinted on the other side and Kiefan was there too.

My breath slowed enough that I swallowed and said, "They mean to wear you down."

"It'll take longer than they think," Kiefan growled, loud enough to tell them all.

Five lamia pinned us down at the fire. The shadows deepened. They darted at Ilya, at me, to make Kiefan spend his kir. Over and over. One got too bold and took a slash across the shoulder. It hobbled into the dark and five became four. But they kept at it.

We heard a shout and an arrow took one beast through the neck. The rest scattered, snarling, and Kiefan rallied with a yell. He wasn't using speed anymore, but they kept well clear of his sword as they fled. Kiefan chased them only a few steps and stopped, swaying on his feet.

Puck's eyes showed whites as he followed Ulf toward the fire; the pony's lead was tied to his belt. A few steps behind, Anders trotted across the clearing and turned to check behind them. Every line on him showed fatigue, the same as Kiefan. Worn down.

I saw the lamia charge from the brush and screamed, throat ragged. Anders' sword spitted one and its impact knocked him down. A second's teeth flashed. Third lamia leaped from the shadows to join in. Kiefan raced across the gap, roaring fury, and the third one kept running. The second broke off and fled too, before our prince's blade was in range.

Ilya rushed to help. I untied Puck from Ulf so he could circle the campfire, arrow nocked and ready. His quiver was half empty, I glimpsed. "Shot that many of them? How many are there?"

His jaw was clenched grimly. "Not all hits. Lamia know about bows."

Ilya put Anders down by the fire and he toppled onto his back, coughing fit to bring a lung up. Blood streaked his sleeve. The boiled leather breastplate had split in two places, at the shoulder, from a pair of punctures.

"He's bleeding," Ilya told me. "His shoulder."

Passing him Puck's reins, I opened my medicine bag. While I knelt beside him, Anders levered himself into sitting up and the effort set him coughing again. His breastplate had stymied half the bite; the other two fangs had torn his left shoulder. I took a blood-stop charm and squeezed it over the wound. The kir unfolded and did its work.

Then I got his cloak off and pulled his cotes aside to see to the rest, as blood-stops did only one thing. I cleansed the bite and asked, "Who else is hurt?"

Kiefan turned toward the fire and I saw his breastplate was gouged with parallel claw stripes. "None of this blood's mine."

Ulf said, "Nothing that needs kir, on me. Just a bandage or two."

"Ilya, give me your kir so I can clear his lungs too," I said, reaching.

"Wait!" Kiefan looked to Ulf. "They're not singing. Will they attack again? How many are left?"

Ulf grimaced. It was true, the lamia weren't singing. "They might. Lamia sing when the hunt's done. As for how many — I wouldn't guess, m'lord. Sometimes we see a dozen at once, but there always seem to be more. We come up here to kill what we can when they get too bold, and we retreat before we lose anybody."

"Save the kir. If they return, I'll need it." Kiefan heaved a sigh. "They've tapped me out."

Anders only twitched a little when I hooked my needle into his flesh. The gashes needed a few stitches of catgut to close them. As I sewed, Ilya asked, "What happened to Acorn?"

I felt Anders tense under my hands. "They hamstrung him. Went for his belly. I cut his throat myself — I wouldn't see an animal eaten alive like that. Let alone a friend." His voice was rough, and he coughed to clear his throat.

"Half our supplies gone," Kiefan muttered.

"Only two days to Vorspitz," Ulf said. "Day and a half if we push hard. If they push hard to reach the fount, perhaps we'll meet them sooner."

Kiefan considered the campfire. "Will they push hard?"

"No secret the lamia will try for weak prey. Especially weak men."

I cut my thread free and Anders sidled his torn cotes back onto his shoulder. Reaching under both layers, I laid my hand on his sweat-slicked chest. "Hope I'm not cold," I murmured, near his ear, and he tried to chuckle. When I called up my kir to clear his lungs, he leaned back against me with a sigh. His kir was tapped out, too, by how little of an answering echo I felt. It took three hard heaves to cough out all his phlegm into the snow, and a little blood came too.

"They took our weakest," Kiefan said, and tensed, spotting something in the darkness. "They're watching still."

"Weakest are taken first." Ulf turned to check on what Kiefan had seen. "Two of them there, yes. It's happened before, to other hunting parties. They whittle away till the strongest is exhausted. Alone. Sometimes that one makes it home, though."

Kiefan's hand went to the leather bag of documents he wore opposite his sword.

I'd never been awake, before, when my day's kir came. At midnight the lamia circled our camp, eyes reflecting the moons and the dim coals the fire had fallen to. Kiefan circled opposite them. Anders and Ulf switched off in joining him. Ilya and I leaned back to back, loosely wrapped in bedrolls, and tried to doze. The lamia would mock-charge, snarling and snapping, just enough to frighten Puck and jolt us all awake. Then they would peel off and meld with the blue snow-shadows.

The day's ration of kir blossomed in my chest, refreshing as a whiff of baking bread to the hungry. We all straightened, we all sighed.

"The saints are with us," Ilya said.

Ulf wasn't as impressed. "With us themselves would be a greater help."

"We're given Blessings to endure trials like these." Kiefan shot a stern glare across the fire at Ulf. "Don't ask Saint Woden to give quarter. He will not."

"As well he's not my saint, then," Ulf returned. "Any who'd care to lend their hand would be welcome, now."

We all glanced up at the cloudy sky, knowing the tales of saints dropping in unexpected. But there was nothing to see.

I caught what sleep I could, the rest of the night. When I saw the Shepherd rising, a thick rind and well before dawn, it confirmed that we'd been gone all the Grain Moon and four days into the Leaf Moon already. I dozed again, longer this time, and woke when Ilya moved to get up. Dawn caught on high, feathery clouds over us. Anders and Ulf stood watch and Kiefan slept, finally, by the fire. The lamia had melted away sometime after moonrise.

Ilya and I packed up what there was of the camp, quietly as we could though Kiefan slept sound as the dead. Anders woke him with a shake, and slipped back Blessing-fast when Kiefan's sword shot up.

"We'll make the fount by noon," Ulf said. "We should skirt it, keep going."

Kiefan still had dark circles under his eyes. "We need the kir. One skin of it could make all the difference."

"They'll be waiting."

"Can you swear they'll leave us be if we skirt the fount?"

Ulf looked away from the challenge. "No, m'lord."

"Then we make the fount by noon."

―――――――――――――――✦――――――――――――――――

Clouds thickened overhead and the frost lingered well past dawn. Winter advanced down the mountainside at night, was pushed back by sunny days but left crusts of snow under the pines. We walked without speaking, Ulf ahead and the knights behind, Ilya and I with Puck in the middle. I had to watch my feet, as my tired mind wandered and missed the tree roots or jutting rocks in the trail. My ankles throbbed from stumbling. My back ached from sitting all night.

And they followed us, a rustle off to one side, a whuffed breath on the other. Puck's ears swiveled to and fro and at first he startled every few minutes, as raw-nerved as any of us. Well before noon came, he merely plodded on, exhausted.

The trail led down a rocky slope that was tricky for a pony. I took Puck's reins and Ilya leaned against his chest to counter-brace and we got him down the first few feet. The fount's pond was in sight and I could feel the kir tugging at me. Puck was looking at it, too, ears perkier than they'd been all morning. He slipped a little and slid against Ilya's weight.

Anders came down a steeper part quickly, sword in hand. "I'll brace his other side."

Ulf stood at the bottom with bow ready, scanning a half-circle. It was only the motion that warned me; they came silently this time, from opposite sides. My scream was entirely too slow. An arrow took one; the other knocked Ulf to the ground.

I was thrown down on the rocks and agony clamped onto my arm. It dragged me like a doll, despite my thrashing against its wiry fur, despite grabbing at whatever passed by. The beast shook me and my shoulder cracked.

That instant it paused to shake, a hand grabbed my ankle and pulled so hard the lamia spun around on my arm despite its claws scrabbling for purchase. A blur of steel and the monster screamed. Kiefan spun around over me, straddling, blade slicing a wide, challenging circle. Lamia fell back on either side, snarling, and he snarled back.

"Come on, you fucking cowards!"

My head spun from the pain and his voice hazed out. Hands dragged me, this time. Blood pulsed under my grip as I clutched my wounded right arm. A hand pried at mine, forced it off. I felt kir pour onto my agony and the distinctive clench and twist of a blood-stop working on my flesh.

"Kate!" Ulf shook me. "Kate, we need you! Ilya needs you!"

The haze parted a little. I had half a heartbeat to glimpse the underside of a grandfather tree's torn-up roots and the shelter it gave us. "Kate, it's Ilya," Ulf told me, pulling me up to sitting. "They tore him bad."

"Use a…" I wobbled, a little dizzy. When I tried to raise my right hand, all I got was pain.

"The charm couldn't stop it."

That jolted me clearer. Ilya lay just beside me, in a spreading puddle. I pulled my medicine bag over my hip and groped in it left-handed. His arm, at the elbow, was a ragged tear that bone peeked through. Blood gushed in time with his racing pulse, slowed by the blood-stop but still draining him.

Too much for a charm, yes, they'd punctured the artery. For all my time in the battlefield surgery, we'd gotten no bleeders like this. They all died on the grass they fell to. I didn't have a memory to call up for this, I realized with a stab of fear.

My hand found another blood-stop, pulled it out. Ilya looked up at me, tear-streaked, eyes crinkled in pain, hissing breath through his teeth. He was pale and weak from lost blood, and still bleeding. I was the only one who could help him.

Tucking the charm under my ring and pinkie fingers, I called my kir to my hand. Ilya's patterns responded, weak and stumbling, his meridian thready. In the raw meat of his arm, my thumb and index finger found the broken artery near the meridian and I pinched it shut.

At a nudge, the blood-stop charm unknotted and this was something I wasn't sure I could do. I focused the charm solely on the one artery, and funneled its kir onto a small clump of whorls with the memory of a freshly cauterized amputation to shape it.

I thought I smelled a bit of singe, but that may have been the memory.

When I let go, the seal held. Ilya's meridian still wavered, above the wound, and below the gash it faded. He'd lose the arm. I couldn't stop that, and I couldn't finish that job either. Not until I could get the hatchet.

Ilya still gasped for breath, terribly pale, his eyes unfocused. I found his pulse in his clammy throat, racing but weak. He'd lost a lot of blood.

"Water!" I looked for Ulf, for anyone, but they stood in a ring, holding off the lamia. Puck was a few steps away, too exhausted to care. One of our water skins lay on the dirt, too — mine, in fact. I tried to get up, got a fresh stab of pain from my own wound that made my head spin, and crawled on my knees instead. Dragging it back, I pulled the stopper with my teeth.

Ilya coughed when I poured water into his mouth, but he swallowed some. He swatted at me, or tried to, and moaned in pain. I saw the charm-hand nub on him and grabbed at his wrist. He tried to shoo me off, but I leaned across and caught him. His day's kir was unspent, I could feel it through his Blessing.

I lost my balance, one-handed, and fell across his broad, heaving chest. "Get off!" he gasped. "Can't breathe... can't..."

Master Parselev had saved a few men who'd come close to dying on the table. Even once the wounds were closed, the lack of blood could kill a man. He hadn't shown me how he'd done it, not in detail, but Ilya didn't have long. I tugged at his kir and it came, rushing out of his Blessing into my arm in a warm glow. My own damaged kir surged as the flood passed through, and I clenched my teeth against the pain.

I remembered the densely packed, dancing whorls of healthy blood flow and poured both Ilya's kir and my own into him.

His body shuddered under me the same moment as I felt my pain slip through my focus, twisting the charm. I grabbed after the kir as it slid from me, its new pattern askew. Caught a handful or two that was still mine, pulled it back. But the tainted charm splashed into Ilya and maimed his patterns, multiplied by a double dose of kir.

He screamed, throwing me off with another convulsion. Ilya clawed at his chest with his good arm, wounded limb feebly scrabbling at the dirt, as I tried to stop him. Ilya was too strong for me to stop him from scratching himself. The charm, set in its faulty pattern, struck his weakened meridians and they sputtered.

I couldn't see for a moment, and then the tears gushed out and the sight of him shuddering with pain cording his throat was too much. With the little kir I had left, I put my palm to his head and struck. Clumsy as a hammer, but it knocked him out.

Ilya went limp, passing out of pain's reach. His voice trailed off as his breath ran out, then turned to a hoarse gurgle in his throat. Still glowing with kir, the meridians around his heart faltered. I bit my lip as I watched my patient, companion, and friend die from my fumbling. I burned it into my memory, tear-blurred, anguished and all.

"Kate?" Kiefan asked, from behind me. "What happened?"

I covered my face with both hands and sobbed.

CHAPTER 12

Lamia lounged by the kir fount, drinking when they pleased and taking turns circling our windfall. A tall pine's roots had torn up a little hollow when it fell, and a smaller fallen tree alongside provided us a bit of low wall.

The sparkling kir and its siren call made my throat all the drier. I had run out of tears after killing Ilya. I could hardly bring myself to speak at all. Somehow, they still trusted me to hold Puck's reins, in the elbow of the roots and the tree trunk. My right bicep pounded under my torn sleeve. Ulf had cut off my layered woolens and I'd wiped the clotted tooth marks with witch hazel. He'd bandaged me. I could move my hand a bit, but kept it tucked in my belt for warmth.

"Two arrows left," Ulf said. "Lost the rest when they knocked me down." He'd used a blood-stop on himself and bandaged his own bites. Wise not to let me try anything, I supposed.

"Save them. Sundown's still a mile off." Kiefan said, intent on the fount.

"There's ten of them, m'lord. It would be suicide."

"They could finish us now, if they wished."

A moment's silence, and then Ulf said, "They're better fed."

I closed my eyes, seeing Boristan dragged off again. And poor Acorn.

Kiefan said, "But they won't let us go."

"No."

Three lamia charged our windfall with more snarls and Kiefan swept Ulf back with one arm. Anders was half a step ahead, counter-charging, and the two knights drove back two of the beasts. The third raced in closest and angled its charge at the last moment, leaping up

113

onto the low tree trunk and running its length, snapping at Puck's head as it passed.

Puck spooked back with a scream and reared. I lost his reins and saw only hooves above me; cringing, I crawled and was nearly hit when Puck came down. The pony dropped his head and I saw teeth; I flinched back under his feet. The men yelled. Puck shrilled and kicked — he'd had enough of all this and who could blame him. I wrapped my arm around my head and looked for an opening, some chance to get out from under his hooves.

Anders caught his bridle; Puck lunged to bite and Anders slapped his palm flat on the pony's forehead, square on his little white star. Kir moved, I felt it. Puck froze, head lifting, ears perked, eyes locked on his. Anders nodded to the pony and took his hand away. Puck whuffed and mouthed his bit. Anders started unbuckling the packs.

I crawled out and stood. Kiefan and Ulf looked as puzzled as I.

And it was an excellent chance to attack us again; two lamia took it, and Kiefan swung around on one of them. It peeled off with a snarl. The second got closer, made to take the same route along the tree trunk as its pack-mate, but Puck lunged with his teeth bared. The lamia spooked, this time, fell off to the outside and scrambled away.

Anders patted the pony's shoulder.

"Could've charmed him earlier," Kiefan said.

"Never did that before," Anders replied, getting the tarp roll off Puck. "You need a horse de-wormed, I know that one. Never tried charming before. He needs the weight off, though. Looks like we're staying here tonight in any case."

———————✦———————

No fire. No camp. The overcast sky blanketed us in shadows quickly as the sun set, and the fount's glow was soon the strongest light under the trees. I wrapped my cloak tight around myself, and sat atop one of the bedrolls we had left. Should the final attack come, being bundled up was no safer than trying to run. Better to not be tangled in a blanket, better to run and be pulled down. A quicker death, perhaps.

What would they tell my mother?

"Kate?" Kiefan's hand found my arm and he knelt beside me. I clasped his hand as the other touched my cheek, cupped it to be sure where I was for a kiss. Then he whispered, "We'll survive this night. And I hope you forgive me for Ilya, someday."

I breathed a bitter laugh. "Forgive you? I'm the one who failed him."

"We should've skirted the fount. You should not have had to overreach yourself."

I stroked his scratchy cheek. "Anything might have happened. You can't say there was no chance he'd be bitten, out here. It was my fault."

He hugged me and I felt a moment's safety; then he went back to the front line.

I sat alone. Ulf had his dagger, and leaned against the sloping tree-trunk to watch for flank attacks. Puck stood guard with him, biting at any lamia who came near. They didn't care to let him succeed. Kiefan and Anders took to letting the mock-charges get far closer before reacting, and killed a couple more lamia thus. The harrying slowed, then.

Pain ground out of my bitten arm, my sprained shoulder. I could feel the swelling, with my left hand, but the joint was still sound. My bandage needed checking, but would have to wait. I focused on clenching my right hand in a fist, wincing and gritting my teeth through the jolts and jabs.

With no moons to track the night's progress, I don't know how much I slept. Puck dozed on his feet and I suspect the men did too.

Sometime before dawn, it began to snow. Wind breathed through the pines' high branches. Flakes pattered down steadily. Snow caught the sparkling kir fount's light and made a misty glow of it.

The silence was nearly peaceful.

"Have you seen any?" Kiefan asked.

Anders jerked awake, I think, on his feet. "No, no sign."

"Only the snow," Ulf said. "Not much night left."

"Give Puck his breakfast, he'll need it. Kate, something for the rest of us?"

There was trail bread aplenty, and cold ham. We drank some water from one of the skins.

"And this is what happens next," Kiefan said as he brushed crumbs from his hands. "Kate takes the documents and some food. She rides Puck. Anders, can you charm him to run till they're safe or he drops?"

Quietly, Anders said, "Don't need a charm for that."

My throat was too tight to speak as Kiefan continued. "We attack. We show these animals what they should be afraid of. And we make an opening for Puck to get through. Ulf? You shoot from up there." He jerked his chin toward the crown of the windfall's roots. "Are we agreed?"

I squeezed out a tiny, "No?"

"You're the smallest. Puck can run the fastest. Would d'Ovio Alain disagree with my logic?" Kiefan asked, referring to the book we'd studied together.

"Don't…" I had packed away my memories of Ther Boristan screaming as the lamia tore at his arms, but I could still picture it all too clearly. Kiefan, Anders, Ulf.

Kiefan hung the leather bag on my shoulder. Ulf put some bread in my medicine bag. I hugged him, and he said something kind, and then I hugged Kiefan longer, tighter. He had to pry me off.

Anders stood with Puck, and dawn was clearly here. The snow had paled to nearly white. He put me on the pony and threw a rope around my waist, then Puck. "Just to be sure," he told me, softly. "Hang on tight. Stay low, there may be branches. I told Puck what I could — horses see things differently. If he stops and you're off the path, find running water and follow it down."

Puck's back put me a little taller than Anders; I caught him with my good arm and hugged him too. He gave me a quick squeeze back and said, "Don't tell anyone you did that."

It seemed ludicrous, given the moment. "I can hug my friends if I wish."

Anders started to tease in return, there was enough light to see that, but it died in his mouth. He only looked at me as he tightened the rope's knots. Then he turned to Kiefan. "Ready?"

"Shepherd, guide my sword."

The lamia clustered around the fount, watching. Kiefan and Anders took deep breaths, crouching to run, steeling their nerves;

116

my hands shook around handfuls of Puck's mane. With a yell, they charged. At Blessing speed, they were halfway to the fount before the lamia could believe their eyes.

The boldest pack-mates answered the charge, and the snow swirled in the wake of two of the saints' Blessed carving through fur and bone.

"Go, Kate! Go!" Ulf shouted.

I kicked Puck hard and he sprinted across the fresh powder. He galloped toward the water, cut right through a gap I barely saw and passed between the pond and the fount. I glimpsed furious green eyes as lamia turned to give chase. One leaped up at the pony's shoulder and an arrow thumped into the monster's neck.

Puck ran into the pines. I threw myself down and gripped his neck as best I could with both arms. Two lamia raced alongside us, on either side, and one suddenly crashed in a shriek and a glimpse of fletching.

Needled branches scratched at me, then vanished. I forced my eyes to open and risked looking up. Puck loped alongside the stream, down the forest path we'd followed up to the fount weeks ago. The way twisted, but wasn't so steep as above the pond. The pony still leaped now and then over little drops and I rattled against him each time.

When he landed, the last lamia slammed into his rump. Claws caught on my cloak and teeth sank in as the beast lost its balance. Puck stumbled, whinnying, and bucked. I yanked at my cloak pins as the lamia's weight dragged at my neck and got them free as it choked me. Puck kicked again as the beast fell, taking my cloak along, and the pony bolted. I checked over my shoulder; the lamia lost a few moments scrambling out of my cloak, and chased. Puck pulled away, though, across a brief flat stretch. He puffed out even clouds of breath.

Puck threw me against his neck when he braked hard, skidded, and I nearly lost my grip. Then the kir hit, like a curtain, and as the pony slid to a stop I was slack-jawed and casting about for the source. Behind me, the lamia shrieked a challenge as it all but sat on its rear to stop.

A massive cougar, all rippling golden hide and hazy kir, charged past Puck up the hill. The cat roared in reply and a bright fist of kir smashed the lamia into a red cloud. The cougar leaped up onto a jut of rock and pirouetted, tail slinging wide for balance, to look back. When his kir-lit golden eyes met mine, I knew he wanted me to follow. I kicked Puck, and he obeyed.

I heard, behind us, more horses and men's shouts. As Puck galloped back upstream I twisted to look. They were a dozen, maybe more, wearing a mix of forest green surcotes and black military tabards and carrying strung bows. They saw me, and Puck, and their shouts got louder. I waved and pointed up the hill, tried to yell back but they couldn't have heard me.

Puck crested the last rise and veered toward the pond. We broke some sort of stalemate and the nearer lamia turned, hackles bristling. Kiefan shouted, "Kate, no!" from beyond the fount and I spotted him, back-to-back with Anders. My mind couldn't grasp why there was a lamia against Anders' leg, in the moment I had before the circling beasts rushed him. The weaker one. And the nearer ones charged Puck. Where was the cougar?

With a hiss, an arrow took one lamia down mid-gallop. The scouting party thundered up and the lamia routed before the onslaught. I turned Puck, kicked him, and we circled tight around the pond, crossed the fount again to reach the two knights first. I sawed at the rope that held me and nearly fell off in haste.

Kiefan snatched me in a brief, rib-creaking hug, and I was babbling at him. "Are you hurt? Let me see. Are you bleeding? Anders?"

One lamia had died with its jaws locked on Anders' thigh, at the knee. His strength drained along with the focus of combat, leaving him a rag doll; Kiefan caught him. Blood dripped from Anders' sword arm as his blade fell.

"Get it off him. Then to the fount," I said, untying my medicine bag.

Kiefan wedged his fingers between fangs and yanked, ripping the lamia's lower jaw off clean. Anders toppled flat as blood gushed free. Bright, arterial spurt stained the grass, sinking my hopes with it. But Kiefan was already dragging him to the fount, and getting help from a rescuer with captain's brasses. I followed.

The kir fount's little pool was barely ankle deep and its diamond glitter quickly shifted to ruby. No time for doubts, nor mistakes.

118

Anders was dying before my eyes. I sat beside him in the kir-water, slopped up a mouthful from the clearer side by the spring, and held his wound in the fast-running flow. Surrounded by raw kir, Anders' whorls and patterns came up strong and colorful, stumbling and broken as they were. The torn meridian pulsed bright as he bled, and I reached into the ripped flesh. My fingers found the artery and pinched it.

My memory raced through all of my surgeries, the handful of medical books, all my master had told me, for what to do. How to fix, not just cauterize. And my mind cleared, calmed, as the fount's kir moved through me. With my other hand, I traced the continuation of the meridian up from his ankle and dug into the wound. Somewhere outside my focus, they were holding Anders down while he screamed.

Both ends of the broken artery in my fingers, I pinched and — they couldn't meet, could they? Torn as they were? I tugged, feeling the kir move around me and into the flesh, coaxed with little massaging circles, and found my pinched fingers touching. The reunited meridian pulsed, weak and stuttering for lack of blood. His skin had gone deathly pale; I called on my kir... my kir?

Around me, brilliant tendrils arced up from the fount, traced across me briefly, and fell back. I called again, and a few more shot out to answer. No surprise I felt buoyant and alert; I brimmed with power.

Blood. Do it right, this time. I focused on Anders' meridian, on his artery and the blood inside, and shaped the kir to match its rushing, whirling pattern. Poured it into him. All of it. It felt like wind, or rushing water, that funneled down to a pinprick at the tips of my fingers and into his artery.

A ragged gasp, and Anders lurched up. Then he wobbled and fell back against Kiefan.

I blinked, dazed by how much I'd spent. A lot of kir made less blood than I'd have thought. The pool's light was gone, its twinkle dulled — though not lost entirely. I could feel kir creeping back into the spring, when I called to it. It would be some time before it was strong again.

"Pull him out. I'll stitch the rest," I said.

"M'lady," the captain breathed, eyes wide. "The Shepherd had him. You —"

From my bag, I dug out a blood-stop and tossed it to Kiefan. "For his arm. Do you need one?" I reached for needle and catgut, and a cleansing charm.

Anders' kir patterns still glowed clearly from the washing, making the job of matching torn edges easier. Someone stuffed a blanket under his head and Kiefan left us both to confer with the captain. I sewed carefully, matching grain to grain as I had when a peasant's hatchet had slipped onto his calf while chopping wood. Anders' knuckles gripped white on his cloak.

I ought to have given him a knock-out. Still failing, even in success. "I'm sorry," I told him.

He laughed, and the tension rolled out of him for a moment. "I'm alive," he said. "I'm the last one you'll need to apologize to."

CHAPTER 13

They found Ulf. What the lamia left of him.

"Just a few dozen yards off," the woodsman reported, gesturing past the roots of the grandfather tree. "He put up a good fight, it looks. Followed a blood trail and found one of them half-dead with his knife in its side."

We all looked up as a second archer passed by, hauling a dead weight: the lamia. Blood darkened its fur, and the final arrow quivered from the dragging.

"Men're wrapping him up to bring. Something to bury, that's good. Something for his wife and the boys." The woodsman nodded.

"I'll speak to Baron Eismann," Kiefan said, voice low as he tracked the dead lamia. "His widow, and Bjorn's, will be looked after."

Two armsmen picked up Ilya's blanket-wrapped body from the hollow we'd sheltered in. My throat tightened, again. They carried him to their own pack horse, slung him over and followed that with ropes.

I stood in the eye of all their activity — seeing to the dead, collecting lamia fangs, filling water skins at the fount — reluctant to move. They asked nothing of me, in any case. I was still full of kir, but the sleepless night and healing Anders left me brain-weary. Unfocused. After the long day's battle at Ansehen, I'd felt this and my master had warned me not to try any charms. Having felt kir slip my fingers, I knew why now.

Two more men came from the brush, carrying a tarp wrapped and tied around — too small a bundle. Too thin. And despite the oilskin, it dripped. My stomach twisted, thinking of those two arrows that had helped me escape. But at least we could bring Ulf home.

"Did you see the cougar?" I asked Kiefan, as we rode down the trail.

"Cougar?" He frowned. "Here? Ulf said lamia drive out any competition."

"I saw a cougar on the trail. A lamia had chased us down, and the cougar destroyed it. When he looked at me, I had to follow — and he was leading the scouts."

"He was, m'lady," the captain put in. "If I may." He slowed his horse from a few steps ahead of us, twisting in his saddle.

"You followed a cougar up this trail?" Kiefan frowned.

The man breathed a laugh, shaking his head. "When a cat walks into your camp during last watch and tosses your bow to you, m'lord, you snap to attention. I'll swear to Father Duty he had a man's hands, when he did it. Not a one of us hasn't heard the stories — Saint Aleksandr can wear a cougar's skin when he pleases — but we never thought to see it. Yes, we followed him, and glad we did."

I'd heard more of Saint Aleksandr the craftsman, castle-builder, bridge-raiser, but I had no reason to doubt the captain. "We're in his debt, then," I said.

Kiefan nodded at that. "But I never saw the cougar. Only you riding up, Kate. You stopped my heart for a moment."

"Father Duty must've been watching. You've barely a mark on you," I said. Some tooth-scratches on his forearms, a few sore spots, and nothing more. His woolens had suffered, but not his skin.

He had no answer for it. "They didn't lack in trying."

We rode for Vorspitz as quickly as the horses could manage. I'd wanted Anders carried on a litter for the trip, so as not to worsen his wound, but he'd refused and Kiefan wanted to be home as quickly as we could. Anders rode tied to one of the scouts — and he hadn't much liked that either, but the grumbling had stopped once the riding worsened his pain.

We made good time and pushed on past dark to reach the town. Baron Eismann waited at his gate, lantern in hand, to greet us. I was so exhausted I nearly fell from the saddle; a stable-boy caught me. Soon as my feet touched the ground, I saw Eismann's physician crossing the gate-yard at a run.

I knew her face, and she knew mine; we all had Saint Qadeem's memory Blessing. Anders lay groggy against his scout's back, and needed careful untying and pulling down. I could smell the blood on his bandage as soon as they laid him on a blanket. The physician put a hand on him, called his pattern, and told the men to wait when they began to pick him up.

Putting my hand by hers, I saw the damage too. "He tore the stitches."

"Men." She pursed her mouth and wove her kir into a charm. The top layer of muscle was worst off — and he'd torn the skin's stitches too. Anders hissed through his teeth as his flesh shifted under the charm.

"I'll re-stitch his skin," I said, reaching into my bag.

"Let me help. You're worn to a shade," she said, through her focus on the charm. "Did he... was his meridian torn? You mended that before he bled out?"

I nodded. Her brows rose and she nodded slowly. "Small wonder the Elect apprenticed you."

The men stood waiting; I could re-stitch Anders inside, with a lamp at hand. When the physician gestured for them to carry him in, I stood along with her. The weight of my bag on my right shoulder, so I could reach in with my left, twisted a sharp breath out of me.

Her hand touched me, called my pattern. "You should've told me," she chided. "Come inside. They've kept some mulled cider on the fire. Let me dull that so you can sleep, at least."

Across the gate-yard, as I went, I saw Kiefan and Baron Eismann looking at Ther Boristan's notebook from the document bag. Then Kiefan closed it with a nod, and the Baron gave a few orders to the captain at hand. They followed us inside. I hoped, for a moment, Kiefan might stop, ask about Anders or me — but they strode on with business to see to. Plans to make.

As they should. I pressed my lips together and looked away. Kiefan was the prince, after all. I had a patient to see to.

I sipped a cup of mulled cider as I re-stitched and re-bandaged, and then a maid led me straight to bed. I dropped onto the mattress fully clothed and instantly slept.

A hand shook me awake far too early. "The sooner we leave, the sooner we're home," Kiefan said.

He was right, but I couldn't help a wince as I sat up; my shoulder stabbed pain at the least weight on it. My eyelids were made of lead. And another day's —

Kiefan kissed my cheek. I turned toward him, startled, as he leaned back. His mouth twisted to one side, for a heartbeat. "Word's been sent to my father. We're expected," he murmured, and stood.

I nodded and got up.

Kiefan took the baron aside again over breakfast. I wolfed down eggs and bread and cheese while the physician checked on Anders again. I had my days' ration of kir, and could charm my shoulder a little more. Enough that it wouldn't pain me all day. It needed a fresh bandage, too. The physician strengthened the stitches in Anders' thigh, but it was too large a wound for her to mend entirely. She didn't think he should ride.

There wasn't much that could stop him once he was full of breakfast, though. I followed Anders into the stable and hugged Puck goodbye around his thick neck. He was more interested in the apple that Anders had smuggled out for him, and I would have understood if Puck had been glad to see us leave without him.

Eismann sent a small escort of the Prince's Guard with us and we changed horses at each village along the way. The frosty morning warmed nicely, but the trees were turning to gold and red. Fields were now half-harvested and stacks of oats stood drying.

Ahead, Mount Woden loomed, snow-capped already, the city on its flank wreathed in chimney smoke. On the jutting promontory, the pale granite castle perched with watchtowers craning to take in the entire broad valley. A little downslope, the neatly arrayed roofs of the Order's campus reminded me of the routine I'd be back to soon enough: patching up patients in the hospital, preparing medicines, studying my master's books, eating in the common hall.

I stole a look at Kiefan, riding a little ahead with his eyes fixed on the castle towers. His home.

I gripped my reins tighter, casting my eyes down with a heavy heart.

APPENDIX

CALENDAR OF MOONS

Each moon is four seven-day weeks, covering one complete turn of the Shepherd moon from new to full and back. The last day of the moon falls on the new (dark) moon. The full moon falls in the middle, and equinoxes or solstices tend to land on the waning half-moon. Once, moons began and ended on Saint-days, but the system is old enough that things have shifted — it pre-dates Wodenberg's saints by quite a bit.

Number	Moon	Event
1	Bitter	
2	Ice	
3	Slush	Spring equinox; Kiefan's Lambing-day on the 25th
4	Spring	
5	Field	
6	Warm	Summer solstice
7	Summer	
8	Fruit	Kate's Lambing-day on the 18th
9	Grain	Autumn equinox
10	Leaf	
11	Hunter's	Jousting tournament starts on the first; Anders' Lambing-day on the 11th
12	Snow	Winter solstice; a new year begins

LAMBING-DAY

One's Lambing-day is the first Saint-day after you were born. If you were born on Saint-day, you were Lambed on the next one. The infant is presented to the Mother and Father, and then the entire Flock of a given Orderhaus before the communal meal. Everyone greets the new lamb with a kiss. Traditionally, relatives and friends bring extra sweets for the meal.

Lambing-days are marked with sweets or small gifts, but they aren't significant until a child reaches twelve and is ready for Blessing by the saints.

ON RANKING KIR-MAGES

Laypeople

Nine of ten people have little or no gift for kir. Perhaps eight of those ten can learn one small charm if they set their mind to it, but no more than that. These folk can only feel concentrations of kir if they are very strong (as in a fount or a highly charged kir-mage) and close by. They can retain a small amount of kir if they are given it through a bond or they drink it from a fount's water. Any more than that will overflow and return to the earth.

Laypeople's overall kir-pattern is the baseline for comparison; on sounding, their kir gives a single, short note like a silver bell.

One in ten people cannot use any kir at all, and are not even able to activate charms bound in small objects.

Disciples

Six in a hundred people are able to master a handful of small charms, usually within a certain area of talent such as healing, combat, or crafting in a particular medium. For example, a low-level healer may know: blood-stop, cleansing, how to patch small areas of kir, and how to untangle pain knots. A low-level fighter may be able to sharpen their reflexes, briefly, strike with unusual force, and resist cuts and bruises with a skin-level kir-shield.

These six disciples can hold a bit more kir than laypeople, and the overall kir-pattern inherent in their bodies is a little denser, a little stronger. On sounding, their kir may give two notes, and will last a little longer. Two heartbeats, perhaps. The difference is subtle, admittedly. Advanced disciples — through skill or experience — may attain a full chord of three notes.

Blessed

Four in a hundred have the talent to be counted blessed. All of the Wodenberg enhancements are examples of one blessed-level charm — a true blessed would have two or maybe three such abilities, and a handful of lesser ones. At this level, the use of kir begins to creep out of the tidy groupings that people like to put kir-mages in. Someone who has largely focused on combat may, at this level, also show some talent for mending, or crafting, or shape-shifting.

The person at this level knows that kir charms are not simple formulas, and can be extemporized to some degree. How successful they will be at trying new things, making it up as they go, etc., varies. They will find their limits, sometimes disastrously.

A blessed, when sounded, will give three notes, maybe four, and sustain for as many heartbeats.

An example of the generalizing of kir ability is the Captain of the King's Guard, Aleksandra Rytsarova. In addition to her saint-given speed and anticipation Blessings, which gave her a head start to her full flowering of ability, she can shield herself with kir, charm her sword, and wields a full complement of "household" charms — spark, flame-snuffing, mending torn fabric, sharpening blades, etc.

Elect

The defining sign of an elect is the ability to draw free kir from other people (barring resistance) and to cast charms on others without touching them.

An elect has a deeper understanding of kir and it responds to him accordingly. Charms become large, complex things affecting the full body. They can collect and hold large amounts of kir, and diffuse it to avoid detection. Grouping elect becomes even more difficult, as they often have multiple areas of expertise.

It's often said that the only limits on a kir-mage are inborn ability and his own wit; the elect are in a position to truly explore the limits of that.

Because of their scarcity and power, politics and control play strongly in the life of an elect. Saints seek them out and bind them, offering training and a steady supply of kir in exchange for loyalty and protection. They often function as gate-keepers for the saints, and as such are the focus of all the kingdom's responsibilities — and luxuries — alongside whatever rulership there may be. Power corrupts, after all, and elect can live for centuries.

Saints

The pinnacle of mastery is both a gift and a curse.

Saints tend to say little about what they're truly capable of, but this much is known: a saint is one who can bind a fount to himself. Thus, the full power of one or more wellsprings of kir are always at his command. And therefore, saints seek out founts, guard them jealously, and surround themselves with kingdoms for further defense.

This is because a saint can be cut off from his fount if another saint severs the binding — which can be done at the source. A saint with no fount is far from helpless, but he's much more vulnerable.

Furthermore, saints target each other in order to harvest their accumulated wisdom and charms. This applies to elect as well — blessed are generally not sufficiently interesting to harvest — and further thins the ranks of the weak, insecure or slow-witted.

Exactly how many saints there are, in the world, cannot be said for certain as they can hide their kir and walk among laypeople undetected.

INDEX OF CHARACTERS, PART I

Alphabetical by family name, then given name. No spoilers.

WODENBERG

Saint Aleksandr, of the Wodenberg Trinity. Crafter and shifter.

Biya, Ter of the Order. Elect Parselev's surgery assistant.

Anders Bockmann, knight, Master of Horse to the Prince's Guard, two-time champion of the king's jousting tournament. Bastard son of King Wilhelm and Baroness Frida Bockmann. Currently nineteen, soon to be twenty.

Brauer, knight and sergeant of the Prince's Guard.

Kate Carpenter, Physician of Wodenberg. Student of the Elect, recently graduated to Physician. Recently turned sixteen.

Meinrad Eismann, knight and Baron of Vorspitz. Advises and provisions the mission. Has a wife and several children, including a teenaged daughter.

Adalrich Haken, knight and duke of Alemannia. Son of King Wilhelm's younger sister, and Kiefan's only cousin. Kate amputated his foot at the battle of Ansehen.

Harold, apprentice blacksmith. Kate was betrothed to him, briefly.

Holly, Ter of the Order. Nurse and a friend of Kate's.

Mechdan Parselev, bound Elect of Saint Qadeem, in service of Wodenberg. Physician of the Order. Attends the royal family as well.

Saint Qadeem, of the Wodenberg Trinity. Philosopher saint.

Ilya Rabskov, servant in Castle Kaltkern. Sent on the mission as a general handyman.

Aleksandra Rytsarova, knight and Captain of the King's Guard. Prince Kiefan served as her squire.

Tomas Seagrace, knight and duke of Englia. Married Kiefan's older sister and has two sons.

Bjornhardt Schutze, knight and margrave of Knapptal. Nearly died in the first battle with Arcea's forces.

Boristan Tolstyev, Ther of the Order. Personal secretary to the abbot. Sent on the mission to document events.

Stanislaus Vysokov, knight and duke of Russe.

Olga Vysokova, duchess of Russe.

Bjorn Waldgrun, woodsman. Assigned the mission as a guide by Baron Eismann.

Johanna Waldgrun, Bjorn Waldgrun's wife.

Ulf Waldgrun, woodsman. Assigned the mission as a guide by Baron Eismann.

Kiefan Weissberg, knight and prince of Wodenberg. Third and only surviving son of King Wilhelm and Queen Mercia. Currently eighteen years old.

Wilhelm Weissberg, fourth of his name, King of Wodenberg.

Saint Woden, of the Wodenberg Trinity. Saint of war.

CAERCOED

Anwyl, servant of House Gwatcyn.

Tannait Broic, bound Elect of Saint Sabh, in service of Caercoed.

Saint Conbarre, saint of Caercoed.

Mohra Fionmaen, Captain of the Tadhlon Guard. Translator and intelligence officer.

Aed Gwatcyn, husband to the Margraves of Tadhlon.

Aifric Gwatcyn, daughter and heir of the Margraves Gwatcyn. The wilder one.

Esgwen Gwatcyn, daughter and heir of the Margraves Gwatcyn. The more polite one.

Leix Gwatcyn, Margrave of Tadhlon and Captain-general to the Crown. Mother of the youngest set of twins.

Lorcana Gwatcyn, Margrave of Tadhlon. Mother of Tiarnan, Aifric and Esgwen.

Tiarnan Gwatcyn, eldest son of the Margraves Gwatcyn.

Saint Sabh, saint of Caercoed.

Tana, stable-master of House Gwatcyn.

OTHERS

d'Ovio Alain. Ancient philosopher of Arcea.

DISCIPLE, PART II
claims laid

SAMPLE

(Text not final!)

CHAPTER 1

I'd slept for a thousand years, the ache in my joints told me, and I could have slept another thousand.

When I opened my eyes, Master Parselev sat at the writing desk near my trundle bed, the tuft at the end of his quill bobbing as he wrote. Late morning light slashed across the spacious guest bedroom. I hadn't seen much of the room when the housemistress brought me in by candle light and pulled out the trundle for me. Now the pine walls glowed in the sunlight, warm and reassuring after the cold blues of the snow.

Parselev glanced over when I sat up; his smile flushed out fans of crow's-feet around his brown eyes. He put down his pen and capped his jar of ink.

"Tell me everything, Kate."

I told him everything: the strange sickness in the mountain pass, Kiefan's headaches, the threat of frostbite, and my failure with Ilya.

My voice fell to a strangled whimper, halfway through that part.

Parselev let me recover. "Thus, your tears at the gate."

Last night, I'd ridden up River Road a half dozen paces behind a lieutenant carrying a lantern and shouting, "Make way! The prince!" For the first time, I'd climbed to the very top of River Road and passed through the outer gates of Castle Kaltkern. The king had been waiting for us, as had Master Parselev and squads of servants. The confusion and noise had fallen away, though, when I saw a lone woman with a candle searching through our riding party, asking questions with hope in her face.

Kiefan had taken her to the wrapped body tied to the spare horse.

"I tried to replenish his blood," I said to Parselev, "but my focus slipped. My own wound tainted the charm. I only gave him pain as he died."

"But you tried it."

"It seemed simple enough." I tugged the blankets up around my chin with a shiver. I sat cross-legged on the straw mattress in only my boy's cote and braies. My master's shoulder bag sat on the rumpled main bed, where he'd slept, and I hoped it contained a fresh shift and dress for me.

"Whenever you spin substance from kir, a great deal of it is needed. Far greater than what results. I checked Sir Anders, and I see you must've worked the charm out for yourself."

I told him about the kir fount and Anders' torn artery, about how I had joined the ends of the artery together. How the kir had arced up when I called, and rushed through me like wind. When I finished, Parselev was nodding and stroking his grey beard as he did when he was pleased.

"And that is why you had to go with them, Kate." Then he twitched his shoulders. "One reason. Need spurs growth. And success is the greatest source of confidence. Even a gifted student might never realize that they can work out healing charms on their own, and shy away from challenges. You know that in your bones now." My master smiled and waved a finger vaguely in the air. "Tell me, do you sense any kir nearby?"

I cocked my head. He finished his cup of tea while I waited, trying to detect any tug of kir in my chest. Taking a deep breath, I called with all my strength.

I felt the echo of a tingle against my breastbone.

"That is the Pool," Parselev said. "Good."

"You know that I can feel it?"

A nod. "I felt it shift when you called. It's deep inside the castle, well hidden. You've grown more sensitive and stronger as well — excellent. When we're elbow-deep in wounded this spring, you will need it."

My chin jerked up, at that. There had been talk of evacuating most of the Order's campus to keep the students safe when Arcea's army marched on the city.

Parselev lowered his voice. "Need spurs growth. Whatever happens, I will be here in Wodenberg if Arcea lays siege, and I mean to have you here with me. You are no longer my apprentice, you are a physician in service of the Order. I want you here as my assistant, not shuffled off to some frostbitten village Orderhaus that needs a physician. I haven't had as strong a student in twenty years, and I mean to see you bloom to your fullest — but," and he raised a hand to further emphasize, "but you must stand your ground and bloom on your own. Which you won't if you allow the others to bully you."

He'd said such things before, because for my first year of apprenticeship I had let the older students foist their scutwork on me. They were my betters, and I was only a peasant girl, and it had seemed natural enough. Master had needed to sit by me, my second year, to be sure I stitched every patient he assigned rather than find me later changing sheets or emptying offal buckets. I could boil bandages and scrub tools with the best of the nursemaid Ters, after all the practice I'd had.

I shivered again, imagining they would send me to a village buried in Starknadel-sized drifts. "I won't, Master."

"No longer your master, Kate." He gave me one of his stern looks to reinforce that. Then he asked, "Do you have other questions on what you saw during your journey?"

I took a moment, during which he collected the handful of papers he had spread out on the desk. "Kiefan's headaches," I said. "Prince Kiefan, I mean to say. I've never seen such tightly knotted kir. And he works even through the pain?"

"Our dear prince," my teacher said, tucking the papers into his letter wallet, "suffers from a recurring affliction. I have seen a scattering of them, in my time, and I've traced it to a flaw in the prime meridian's roots which causes the kir to tangle. The tangles catch on his two adjacent Blessings and, when emotions run high, swiftly develop the tight knots you observed."

"There's no way to repair the flaw?"

"There has been no injury to the prime meridian, as the flaw was inherited, in many cases, from one's bloodline. And it's not for any to say how one's mind should be, whatever you might hear otherwise." Parselev stood, with his letter wallet, and lapsed out of his lecturing tone. "I'll let you dress — your clothes are in the bag there. You have a patient to see to, do you not?"

I nodded, but had to ask. "Surely His Majesty couldn't hide such headaches for his entire life?"

He hesitated before answering. "You're my student and I am physician to the royal family. You will be attending to them as well, so in confidence I will tell you that it's the Queen who also suffers a flawed meridian and the headaches. A fact I did not learn until she'd lived here nearly five years, lest you think the prince exceptionally stubborn. Now, I'll see if I can find us some breakfast. Meet me in the hall or down in the kitchen."

———————————✝———————————

Castle Kaltkern lay in rings, its keep and watchtowers on the promontory's peak. From the gatehouse on the innermost wall, the castle's road dropped steeply into an herb garden, wound past a few fruit trees and then the guesthouse Parselev and I had roomed in.

We followed the road outward through the gatehouse in the second ring. I looked up as we walked under the portcullis, wondering at the lattice of iron.

Down another slope we walked into the bustle of the royal stables and the broad yard inside the third, outermost ring. Four wagons stacked high with ale barrels stood in the yard, their lead teamster arguing with a man in servant's blacks about the tally and why it was short. The other teamsters lounged on their wagons, waiting for leave to drive up to the castle proper.

Tucked against the wall, past the stables, was the royal guardsmen's barracks. King, queen and crown prince had their own guard, each with castle duties to see to.

As Parselev and I strolled past the ale wagons, a pageboy in messenger's red sprinted past us, calling for a horse. A stable hand led one out by the reins and the page vaulted into the saddle with ease. At a kick the horse burst off at a canter through the outer gatehouse, hooves echoing off the deep walls.

He nearly collided with two horses trotting in. The man leading the way twisted in his saddle to shout after the racing pageboy. By the fur-lined, dark green cloak, the man was titled, and by the sword he wore he was knighted too — and by how his lean, bearded face darkened, furious. He dismounted before the stable hand could catch his bay's bridle, and fumed toward the stables shouting for Schwartzman. He didn't stay to see his lady off her horse.

She dismounted with ease, though, green skirts and all, and nodded thanks to the stable hand. Then she spotted my teacher and me, nearly across the gate yard by then. Parselev stopped.

"M'lady, it's good to see you well," he called.

"It's kind of you to remember, Elect." She crossed to us at a brisk walk, smiling. The morning sun, just full over the castle walls and flooding the yard, shone on flaxen hair netted up in a dark crespine. I didn't doubt that as a girl she'd been beautiful and kind; she still was, though now seasoned by years. A few lines had gathered around her eyes, but they still twinkled with spirit. "This must be your apprentice?"

Parselev presented me with a sweep of his hand. "My student only, as she's been graduated by Saint Qadeem himself. Dame Kate Carpenter, physician. Kate, the Baroness Rossweide, Frida Bockmann."

Anders' mother. I curtsied, thankful I was back in skirts to do it properly. "M'lady, I'm honored."

"A pleasure to meet you, Dame Kate. I suppose we are at the same purposes," Dame Frida said with a glance toward the stables that her husband had vanished into. "Is he well? His message was too brief." She walked toward the barracks and Parselev fell into step beside her. I trailed, hands clasped.

"Ask his physician," my teacher said, turning to me as he walked.

Frida's brows shot up, startled. "Your pardon, Dame Kate. They dragged you up the Eispitzen for this lamia hunt?"

For most, that was the story we were to tell of our journey. "The Elect knew it would be excellent training for me," I said. "Anders should recover without trouble, m'lady. Sir Anders, I mean to say."

We paused at the sill of the barracks' double doors, which stood open on this fine autumn morning. She smiled with a familiar wry twist. "He said as little in his message. And if you spent the whole moon a-hunting, little wonder if you're on familiar terms. My son, please, Lieutenant." That last to the officer who snapped to attention, fist over his heart, beside the duty ledger's table inside the door. "I'm told you have him here. Sir Anders Bockmann?"

"He's asleep in the Prince's Guard room, m'lady. I'll fetch him —"

"No mind, sir, I can manage that much. See to your work. Which room?"

With directions, we climbed a spiraled stone stair and Parselev put a hand on my shoulder to slow me. "Let a mother see her son first," he murmured.

So we lagged a bit behind her along the hallway. M'lady Frida paused at the door to listen — this late in the morning, the upstairs was empty — and pressed the latch. She leaned to look, and then stepped inside.

"Is it true Anders is the king's son?" I whispered.

"You didn't know?" he asked, but then answered himself. "It's of little matter to us, in the Order. Yes, to the gossips' joy, he is. He is also a fellow disciple of the saints, sworn to their service."

I couldn't help thinking of the tall, lean Baron Rossweide with grey-touched brown hair and beard as he strode across the gate yard. Then, the king when I'd swung down from the saddle last night: blonde-bearded, built for the heavier muscle that he still carried despite being much the Baron's elder. The resemblance was more than the jawline that I had noticed earlier; Anders' whole frame matched the king's.

Near the door, I stopped and waited without looking in.

"I came with your father," Frida said, inside, "but he got no further than the stables."

Anders snorted. "You could've come alone. I have no father."

Her tone steeled. "You'll both be fools if you cast away all your good years over a few head-buttings. He'll take you on as a trainer if you'll only mind the manners I know I taught you. Room and board and working with the horses. Don't try to pass that off as a fleeting fancy to me. You love those horses."

"Trading one hayloft for another," he muttered.

"Will and Ein miss you. And nobody's safe near Nipper. Bring this wound of yours home and recover your strength. Though I must admit you look well — it must be only a slight injury? Why has your physician has come to check on you, then?"

Parselev, on cue, pushed the door open. M'lady Frida sat on the foot of Anders' cot and he'd sat up under the blankets. The other cots stood empty and neatly made. His tabard, mail and gambeson were thrown over a small chest against the wall; he wore only the off-white wool cote and braies from underneath all that.

"Come to check on me? There's nothing to see."

"Let your physician be the judge of that. Show us this trifling wound, then," his mother said, standing up from the cot.

I took her seat as Anders kicked the covers off his right leg. He wore full-length braies, against the cold, and rolled one leg up above his knee. Browned blood stained the bandage. I shooed his hands away and untied it myself.

"Eismann's physician told you not to ride," I said.

"I wasn't about to come home tied to a saddle." He leaned back against the pillow and the wall, content to let me unwind the bandage.

"If you tore those stitches and the wound's set, you'll have a limp."

He didn't answer that as the stained cloth fell free. The lamia had latched onto Anders' thigh just above the knee and shook as it died, leaving a matched pair of gashes as long as my hand. My top stitches, done in plain wool thread, looked as rushed as I had been in making them.

"Those — are no minor wound," m'lady Frida said, voice low. "Anders, what happened?"

I laid my palm against his skin between the wounds and called his kir. His meridian pulsed strong and clear, and most of the wound was beginning to knit, hurried along by the healing charms. But there were patches of kir that followed their own dance striated through his whorls. Left on their own, they'd become abscesses.

"One lamia got under my guard and put his fangs in me. Locked his jaws and I couldn't get the bastard off even dead. Then I heard the scouting party arrive, and..." He shrugged it off with a shake of his head.

"And?" Frida's tone sharpened.

"And here I am."

Sharp enough to cut, she said, "Don't you try to dodge — "

"The Shepherd's shadow fell on me." Anders turned harsh. "I felt his culling knife on my throat. And like a fool, I begged the Mother and Father for one more chance. Swore on my Blessings to both of

142

them." He raked a hand through his hair, pressed the heel of his palm against the fore-nubs at his hairline.

His mother turned to me, her sky-blue eyes bright with pain. "What happened?"

He'd left off the part where the lamia had harried us for two nights. He'd likely run out of kir and that was how the beast got under his guard. But I stuck to the question of the wound. "He lost too much blood while I repaired his meridian. The Shepherd nearly took him. "

Her knees wobbled and she sank to the floor, green skirts puffing out as if to catch her. She held Anders' free hand to her cheek and whispered, "Mother Love, thank you… thank you, Saint Qadeem, for your disciple."

I worked through the clotted lines of kir and the young abscesses in his wound. By how he winced, he felt me undoing the damage his day's ride had done to the interior stitches. I didn't have enough kir to repair it all, but did enough that he wouldn't have a limp.

"I will need to check the wound again and remove these stitches," I said, tapping the wool threads. "In a week or so."

"Come by whenever you wish, Dame Kate," m'lady Frida said, wiping her eyes. "Be welcome in my house whenever you wish a good meal."

From the door came a new voice. "What did you swear?"

Parselev waited just inside the sill. Beside him stood the Baron Rossweide with arms folded.

Anders heaved a sigh. "To the Discipline. To submit to their Discipline."

The baron snorted at that. "You haven't the stomach for either of their Disciplines. That much is clear from the past few years. Culling knife, indeed."

"I'll keep my word."

Another snort. "Your mother wants you home to heal. You won't be under my roof a moment longer unless you earn your keep — and keep for that damn horse of yours."

"I'll be in the training yard at dawn, then," Anders said, his voice gone cold. "Once I've seen to duties here."

"You do that." Turning on his heel, the Baron stalked out.

"The Father's Discipline would go far toward mending bridges between you," m'lady Frida said. "And the Mother's…"

"I was a fool to swear." Anders shook off her hand and leaned out to reach for his gambeson. "I've the Guard's horses to check."

Parselev spoke up. "And debriefing with the King's Council and a funeral tonight."

"Let me bandage that." I put a hand on his wounded knee to stop him, digging through my medicine bag with the other.

Anders pulled the padded tunic to the side of the bed, but waited for me to wrap him back up. "Me, at the King's Council? That will be interesting. If I don't turn up at Ilya's funeral, don't expect to find my corpse."

DISCIPLE, PART II
COMING IN EARLY 2013